Praise for *Daughter of Blue City*

"A deeply moving coming-of-age novel." – **Derrick Meade**

"Impossible to put down." – **TQ Pub**

"What touched me most was how her mother and sister gave her quiet strength." – **Sammy Moon**

"I wasn't ready for the intense emotional reactions this book brought me to. Amazingly strong FMC and the storyline was beyond encapsulating. I was transferred into this character and went through this journey with her." – **Harley Grace**

"This is a fantastic story that pulls you in and shows you to never give up. You feel for the character so much and what she goes through. A truly touching story that I highly recommend!" – **Diana Kimak**

"My heart goes out for young Lianlian. This is a fascinating story of an impoverished Chinese family during the Cultural Revolution." – **John K. Kelly**

"This is a deeply moving and unforgettable story that captures both the heartbreak and resilience of a young girl that truly touched me. This book isn't just historical fiction; it's a reflection on hope, perseverance, and the power of the human spirit." – **John Spender**

Recognitions

ii

- **The 2025 Goethe Book Awards for Post-1750 Historical Fiction:** Long-listed

- **The 2025 Best Book Awards (22nd Annual Awards by American Book Fest):** Finalist for Multicultural Fiction

Daughter of
Blue City

By Apple An

Fiction

Mother of Red Mountains

Daughter of Blue City

Memoir

Las Crosses

Nonfiction Anthology

28 Voices

37 More Voices

Nonfiction Self-Help

All-in-One Dotted Journal Notebook

Daughter of Blue City

A Novel of Coming-of-Age Through
Revolutionary China

Apple An

Voices Heard Publishing, LLC

Museum photo by Jade Bai

Cover design by 100Covers.com

Library of Congress Control Number: 2025917547

ISBNs:

eBook: 978-1-958900-18-5

Paperback: 978-1-958900-19-2

Hardcover: 978-1-958900-20-8

1st Edition, 1st Printing: August 2025

2nd Print: November 2025

For my sister
For my teacher in middle and high school

ACKNOWLEDGEMENTS

I am deeply grateful to everyone who helped make this book happen.

I thank my beta readers Mary Jumbelic, Cynthia Levesque, and Susan Wright. Their candid reactions and suggestions improved the book tremendously.

I owe gratitude to my editor Elisabeth Blair for her diligent, thoughtful, and skilled work on developmental and copy editing that made the book shine.

I thank my dear and brave sister Jade for her unwavering love. She continues to be a solid rock in my life.

My special appreciation goes to Jim Emery, the first and last reader of my stories, my co-conspirator, and my sounding board.

Author's Note on Names

Chinese characters convey both meaning and sound. English transliterations into the Latin alphabet represent only the sounds of the characters—it can be especially difficult to capture the richness of Chinese names, which usually contain multiple characters with layered meanings.

This book uses the following conventions:

People's Official Names:

A man's official name could have three characters in the following order: surname, generation name, and given name. All members of the same generation within a family or clan might share a generation name. A hyphen connects the generation and given names, e.g., Xi-Chang, Xi-Dan.

Traditionally, women didn't have generation names. Some women keep their surnames after marriage, while others adopt their husband's surname.

Names for Babies and Children:

It is common practice to double syllables in names for babies or young children. For example, Lianlian and Shanshan. These doubled names can sometimes become official names when the children grow into adults.

Names for Roles:

The book may use Chinese names to refer to family roles. When these names are used by or for children, the syllables are often doubled without a hyphen. For example:

- Paternal Grandfather: Ye (Yeye)

- Paternal Grandmother: Nai (Nainai)

- Mother: Ma (Mama)

- Father: Ba (Baba)

- Uncle from father's side: Shu (Shushu)

- Older sister: Jie (Jiejie)

- Younger sister: Mei (Meimei)

Names for Places:

Chinese places—such as cities, provinces, organizations, and stores—often have multiple characters that show the type or meaning of the place. Some names become widely recognized as a single concept; for example, few people think of the literal meaning of Beijing ("Northern Capital").

For consistency, one English word is used to represent the sound of a place name, even if the original Chinese name has multiple Chinese characters. For instance, Chifeng refers to a city whose two-character name means "Red Mountains," and Xishanwan means "Valley of the West Mountains."

CONTENTS

PROLOGUE

It was 1977 in Hohhot, the capital of China's Inner Mongolia Autonomous Region. Early fall was a favorite season for the locals—neither hot nor humid, with sunshine filling the long days.

Joyful anticipation filled the air as people looked forward to the positive changes following the end of China's Cultural Revolution a year earlier.

A railroad worker had noticed a particular teenage girl twice now in the late afternoons. She was skinny, dressed in oversized clothes handed down by grown-ups. A schoolbag slung across her body showed she was coming from school. Her two braided pigtails were a typical hairstyle for young girls.

The girl walked along the tracks. He had seen her yesterday and wanted to warn her to stay away, but a co-worker called him away. Before he could get back to her, she had vanished.

Today, he wanted to make sure he reached out and talked to her.

"Hey, young lady, stay right where you are!" The worker hurried toward her, one hand holding the wrench he used to inspect the tracks, the other holding his protective helmet.

The girl paused and turned. Her gaze was vague, fixed on a distant point.

The worker took a deep breath—her face showed no fear, only deep sadness. Something heavy weighed on her mind.

"What are you doing here?" he asked.

The girl snapped back to the here and now; her expression shifted from sad and desperate to alert. She replied, "Just walking."

"How did you get in here? This area is dangerous; it's for workers only."

She pointed at the large metal gate for moving luggage carts.

"Through there," she blushed.

"Little girl, what's your name?" the worker asked, his tone free of blame and full of concern.

The girl looked at him, hesitating, then replied softly, "Zhou Lianlian. My name is Zhou Lianlian."

"Zhou Lianlian, which school do you attend? Which grade?"

The girl still showed no fear. His kind expression and gentle tone must have assured her he was trustworthy.

"Hohhot 2nd Middle School. I've just started the third year."

The worker thought she was small for that grade. "That is 25 minutes from here. Where do you live?"

The girl took a slow, steady breath before responding. "About five minutes from here," she said, adjusting her schoolbag to give her right shoulder a moment's relief.

"I... I used to come here to watch the trains with my sister."

The worker nodded and looked her over carefully. He believed she was telling the truth, and his voice became even gentler.

"You should go home now. This is not a place for members of the public. Last week's accident caused us a lot of grief. Poor boy. He would still be alive if he hadn't come here to play with his buddy. You must have heard about the accident?"

The girl nodded, glancing down at her feet for a moment before lifting her head. "Sorry to cause you concern. I was just walking and thinking. I'll go home now," she said.

"Good. Don't come back again. Let me lead you to the gate."

PART I

FAMILY OF FOUR. 1966–1973

1

LIANLIAN'S FIRST MEMORIES

966 saw the beginning of the Cultural Revolution. The nation was in a state of widespread unrest.

In Hohhot, known as the Blue City for its vibrant blue sky and dark blue mountains, a tragedy was playing out.

"Mama! Mama! Shushu! Stop it! Stop it!" Three-year-old Lianlian screamed.

Two uncles held Mama down before her. Uncle Shorty pinned Mama's arms over her head. Uncle Naughty perched on top of her, striking her face and upper body.

Mama fought to break free, shouting, "You bastards! You bastards!"

With each slap, angry Uncle Naughty yelled, "Liu Jun! We'll teach you a lesson!" "You're a traitor to our family!" "You broke my ma's heart!"

Uncle Shorty hollered, "Hard! Harder!"

"No! No! Shushu! Stop! Stop!" Lianlian shrieked. Mama tried to turn her head to face the little girl but couldn't move. Uncle Shorty was about to strike her, but just then Mama freed her hand and hit his nose, drawing blood. In return, he punched Mama hard, then grabbed her wrist again to hold it down.

"Nooo!" Lianlian whimpered. A warm liquid gushed down her legs all the way to her feet. She longed to be near Mama, but her legs were too heavy to move. She tried to raise her voice, but she couldn't hear herself shout.

Shanshan, her two-year-old sister, crawled up to her big sister and screamed, "Mama! Waaaaa! Bad Shushu! Bad Shushu! Waaaaa!"

Lianlian looked around. Scared and desperate, she cried out, "Baba! Baba! Where are you?"

Later at the hospital, Aunt Long, their daytime babysitter while Mama worked, led her and Shanshan to a white room containing a single bed. From afar, Lianlian could make out a form shrouded in white.

Aunt Long whispered to the girls, "Shh. Mama is sleeping. Don't wake her."

"That's Mama?" Lianlian pointed to the figure in disbelief.

Aunt Long nodded and led the girls inside to sit on the floor beside the bed and play with a length of yarn. The endless patterns they could make with it could keep the girls busy for hours under normal circumstances. This time, though, Lianlian kept her eyes fixed on Mama.

When Mama made a noise, Lianlian sprang up to stand by her bed. Aunt Long lifted Shanshan and put her in bed next to Mama. Shanshan touched Mama's good hand and pointed to Mama. "Mama! Your face!"

The visceral memory of her two uncles hitting Mama came back to Lianlian. Tears swelled in her eyes, and though she tried hard not to, she started sobbing. Shanshan joined in, and the girls' wails filled the room.

Jun tenderly stroked the girls' heads with her good hand. "Shh, babies. Don't cry. Mama will be home soon."

Two days later, when Aunt Long brought them home, Lianlian met a towering figure at the door. He scooped up Shanshan and then beckoned to Lianlian.

It's Baba! But Lianlian felt distant from him, as if he were a neighbor or her parents' colleague.

Where had he been? Why hadn't he been home to stop Shushu?

Baba kept waving, but Lianlian didn't move. She looked at Mama, whose face remained wrapped in white gauze, then turned back to him and saw his expression change from happy to unhappy. That frightened Lianlian.

Will he beat Mama too if he's unhappy? Will he beat me?

One month after Baba came back, he was gone again. Shanshan was playing with a piece of fabric. Jun sat on the kang (a built-in bed made of bricks and mud for the entire family to sleep on) to sew a button back onto a shirt. Beside her, Lianlian's eyes traced the motions of Mama's hands.

"Mama, what is a bastard?"

Startled, Jun peered at Lianlian, then said, "It is a bad word for a bad person."

"Like Shushu?"

Jun closed her eyes for a moment. "Yes, they are bad because they attacked me."

"I don't like Shushu."

Jun paused a moment again. "Do you remember playing with Uncle Naughty in Yeye and Nainai's house?"

"No."

"How about Uncle Shorty, who brought yummy food for you and Shanshan?"

"No."

"Do you recall Yeye and Nainai?

"Yes."

"Can you recall visiting their house and the fun you had there?"

"No."

"Oh well, you were very young. You're still young. Your uncles are not always bad. They were angry with me. Now, take your shirt off so I can mend that tear."

For over a decade, Jun—and later Lianlian—spent countless mornings airing damp bedding in the summer sun or by the winter stove.

One morning, Jun scolded Lianlian. "How many times have I told you not to drink water before bed?"

But I didn't, Lianlian thought to herself, feeling wronged and helpless. She understood her mom must be frustrated, but she was, too.

Another morning, Jun was more compassionate. "It's not your fault. You were well potty-trained for nighttime by the time you were just one year old. You only started bed-wetting after you saw your two uncles beating me."

Lianlian tried to hide the wetness by drying it with her body heat during the night, but it seldom worked. Hanging bed sheets in the yard was like raising a surrender flag. It provided another reason for people to laugh at her and her family.

Jun explored different ways to cure Lianlian's bed-wetting. When she was in elementary school, Jun took her to a clinic.

Lianlian saw the long silver needles and clung to Jun.

"It's OK. It won't hurt. See?" Jun extended her free hand and gestured to the acupuncturist to insert a needle into her hand.

Lianlian obeyed the instructions to lie on the bed and endured the needles being inserted into her arms, legs, and belly button. The final needle went into her scalp. Her mom was right—there was no pain. But it didn't work, regardless of the number of sessions.

A different doctor recommended Chinese medicine. After boiling dried herbs in a special pot, Jun brought a bowl to Lianlian. The horrible odor and the bitterness it left on her tongue made Lianlian nauseous.

Jun instructed Lianlian, "Hold your nose and don't take breaks. Finish the whole bowl in one breath."

Pinching her nostrils, Lianlian emptied the bowl. Then, with tears streaming, she promptly threw up, making a big mess. Countless tortures later, Jun gave up.

Nothing had worked until Lianlian began menstruating in middle school. Without doing anything, the bed-wetting mysteriously stopped. However, she never forgot the shame and self-loathing.

Years later, when Lianlian was fourteen and in high school, she recounted her first memories to her mother, hoping to learn more details of the assault.

"Mom, why did Uncle Shorty and Uncle Naughty beat you? When exactly was that?"

"It was 1966, at the beginning of the Cultural Revolution. You were three, Shanshan was two."

"What was the Cultural Revolution really for?" Lianlian had heard so much about it, but she hadn't quite internalized it.

"It was supposed to eliminate capitalists and other old elements of society."

"Why did that have anything to do with uncles beating you?" Jun searched for the right words.

"It's a little complicated. Yeye and Nainai took care of you and Shanshan because I worked full-time, and your father was always away from home. Then, the Red Guards raided their home several times."

"Is that because Yeye had been classified as a capitalist?Lianlian knew he had been a successful Jinzhou entrepreneur before 1949.

"Yes—and no. All capitalists were targets at the beginning. But Nainai made it worse."

"Why?"

"Nainai never understood why her family had become a target, given all the good things Yeye had done. She was proud, disagreeable, and uncooperative. She didn't give a damn what the Red Guards said. Her poor attitude really antagonized the Red Guards. They came by often and destroyed the property and belongings."

"Were you ever there for those raids?"

"Yes, several times. I missed you two and made frequent trips to visit you. One visit prompted my decision to remove you."

"What happened?" asked Lianlian.

Jun took a deep breath.

"The Red Guards pushed your grandparents into the center of their yard. The neighbors and passersby gathered around to watch. Nainai was holding Shanshan, and you were in Yeye's arms."

Jun paused and drank some tea. It was hard to put her memories into words. Seeing Lianlian's curious eyes, she continued.

"A young Red Guard ordered Nainai to lower her head and let him put a dunce hat on her head. Nainai refused."

Lianlian could just picture Nainai doing that. She recalled a visit to her grandparents in 1971 when she was eight. Nainai had been an intimidating old woman, who seemed irate and rigid. But it was because she had cancer and suffered great pain.

"Several Red Guards got hold of her and shouted slogans. You and Shanshan were terrified and cried hard. I asked Uncle Shorty to take you both from your grandparents. But he refused and said the Red Guards would go easier once they saw the babies crying."

"Did the Red Guards go easy? Did it work?"

"Not that I saw. That's when I decided you two needed to be away from your grandparents' house, at least for a while."

"But how did you take us away? You were a young woman, and the two uncles still lived at home."

"I went to the Red Guards' headquarters to seek help. A group of them accompanied me. They held guns to ensure the family stayed put while I escorted you both away from the house and to the train station. Your grandparents and two uncles were furious, but they couldn't do anything."

Lianlian's admiration of her mother's bravery and intelligence skyrocketed.

"Your grandparents' family hated me and considered me a traitor to the family. That's why your uncles came and beat me, even in front of you two."

"Bastards! I hope I never see them again."

Lianlian gritted her teeth. The image of her mom being beaten by two uncles would stay fixed in her memory forever.

After a pause, she asked, "I thought the uncles adored Father—how could they beat his wife?"

"They wouldn't have dared if your father was present."

"I wish he weren't my father." That sentiment was based on much more than Lianlian's earliest memories.

2

JUN'S DETERMINATION

"How did this happen? How could things have gotten this bad?"

Once she regained consciousness after that attack by her two brothers-in-law in front of her baby girls, Jun went over and over these questions thousands of times in her head.

Until 1966, life had proved difficult, yet manageable. Her parents-in-law took care of the babies in their Jinzhou home so that Bin-Kai and Jun could focus on their jobs—both of them worked at a government-owned civil engineering institute for designing dams and bridges.

Constructed in the early 1950s in Hohhot, the capital of the Inner Mongolia Autonomous Region, the institute was top-ranked in the country. It hired top talent from leading universities, such as Tsinghua University (Bin-Kai's alma mater), and top vocational schools like the one that trained Jun.

Jun had never dreamed of joining such a prestigious institute. She'd traveled from her hometown, Chifeng, to Hohhot to continue her studies at the vocational school. Her parents had died, and her older brothers had left home. She and her younger sister, Xia,

15

survived by living in a schoolroom. There was no money left for her to finish high school and then go to college. The vocational school was her only choice because it enabled her to fund herself and even save money for Xia to use.

Disciplined and competitive, Jun distinguished herself both in political correctness and in academic competence. In 1959, she was the only graduate from the vocational school chosen to join the institute.

Jun's career was flourishing. She had been an outstanding engineer, capable and reliable. No one had questioned her political views. Her superiors informed her that consistent effort and performance could lead to Communist Party membership, boosting her career and respect.

Jun and Bin-Kai fell in love in 1961, when she was drifting away from her middle-school sweetheart. However, an unplanned pregnancy and the belief that Bin-Kai didn't love her caused her the utmost shame and anguish because she was afraid of ruining her reputation and career. The institute's leadership intervened and turned a potential suicide into a marriage.

Lianlian's birth in 1963 changed Jun's in-laws' reaction to her from hostile to welcoming. They even offered to help raise Lianlian, but Jun declined.

Jun was a young mother and a star engineer, while Bin-Kai was often out of town at remote sites. She had to quit volunteering (she'd been leading the Communist Youth League and organizing various activities). But her work was on the same level as that of top engineers in her field, and she continued to receive praise and promises from her leaders.

Shanshan arrived one year after Lianlian. Jun was overwhelmed. She didn't think it was possible to take care of two babies and keep a demanding job. She turned to her parents-in-law, whose offer still stood. Bin-Kai took Shanshan to his parents' home just days after she was born. The whole family then endured six months of hell after Shanshan contracted meningitis and nearly died.

After Lianlian and Shanshan became inseparable, Bin-Kai's parents took Lianlian in, too.

Jun's last visit to the girls and her capitalist in-laws at the onset of the Cultural Revolution changed everything.

Jun had to protect the scared girls. Constant Red Guard visits and her in-laws' inability to offer protection prompted her to remove them from her in-laws' house. It was an action based on a mother's instinct, a decision with no room for debate.

The consequence? This brutal violence, inflicted by her brothers-in-law, who used to adore her beauty and intelligence.

Should I have chosen differently? Should I have left the girls in their care and allowed the Red Guards' chaotic, repeated visits to keep scaring and traumatizing them? No way. I'd do it again! I'd take them away in a heartbeat, given the chance to do it over.

Jun hadn't expected the damage her actions might have caused to the in-laws. She knew they were good-hearted people and loved the girls. She appreciated that they'd been a tremendous help when she and Bin-Kai struggled to meet the challenge of juggling both parenting and work.

The head of her division suggested she should report the beating to the police.

But what then? Adding this event to their records could ruin the young men's lives forever. They would never find decent jobs. And my parents-in-law? They'd lose their granddaughters and then their sons. What if the authorities released them? What would be the potential consequences? They'd become my enemies for life.

No, I cannot report it.

Bin-Kai was hit hard by a wave of shock when he rushed home. But it didn't stop him from caring for her and the girls. He didn't blame her for what she'd done. He didn't show any sign of abandoning her and the girls. Although there was still no way of knowing what would happen next, Jun knew she needed to care for the girls herself.

From now on, my children are my top priority, and work comes second, she resolved.

3

BIN-KAI'S STRUGGLES

It was the fall of 1966, and Bin-Kai had been home for the past week. Since he had joined the institute five years ago, this was his first extended period of staying home to work. The institute assigned male and childless female engineers to work on projects in distant, uncivilized locations for weeks or months.

Ten days ago, a telegram had reached him at his remote location: "Emergency at home. Return ASAP." The most affordable way to send a telegram was to use the smallest number of words possible. With no details, Bin-Kai had worried sick during the two-day trip back home.

He couldn't believe his eyes when he opened the door. Gauze covered the head, right arm, and right hand of his beautiful, intelligent, and capable wife, with whom he had fallen in love at first sight. The exposed skin on her face showed bruises. Her eyes were pink with dark eyebags. She must have had a pain in her chest because her left hand was covering it.

Bin-Kai immediately thought of beating whoever had done this to her. To his astonishment, his two youngest brothers, 18 and 24, who adored him and his wife, had been the culprits.

More and more questions came to him as he learned. But Bin-Kai's priorities were Jun and the girls, and pressing local projects, since his remote work had to be completed in-house.

Each day he rose, got breakfast, fed his family, and then transported his daughters to Aunt Long's on his way to work. At midday, he got lunch for Jun and himself, napped, and then resumed work. He relied on the canteen again for dinner for the whole family.

One day, after finishing dinner, Bin-Kai said, "I asked Lao Wang for a few days to visit my parents."

Jun nodded. "It's time to check on them. I can take care of myself and the girls."

Bin-Kai was relieved to see Jun making a slow and steady recovery. Having him at home had been a real comfort for her. She had talked about resuming work once the facial wraps were gone and her hand could hold pencils.

"I'll catch tomorrow's train then."

He busied himself with household chores and didn't notice that Lianlian and Shanshan had gone outside to play on a side road near home.

A three-wheeled cart lost control and crashed into the girls. One wheel ran over Shanshan's throat and cut her face. Shanshan shrieked, then fell silent. Lianlian escaped. She screamed for her parents.

Bin-Kai sprinted outside in a few big steps. He picked up Shanshan, examined her, and shouted to Jun, "I'm taking her to the hospital!" With Shanshan in his arms, he ran to the hospital.

Jun and Lianlian arrived later.

Shanshan lay in bed, her eyes closed. Gauze covered her head, apart from around her eyes and mouth. Bin-Kai sat in a chair next to the bed, his body doubled over, his head in his hands.

Lianlian let go of her mom's hand and hurried to Shanshan's bed. She looked at Shanshan, then her father, then Shanshan again. "Baba, will Meimei be home soon?"

Bin-Kai raised his head; his eyes filled with worry and pain. Without a word, he lifted Lianlian and spanked her bottom.

"No. She'll be here for days—and it's your fault. You should have taken better care of her—you're her big sister!"

Jun jumped up to grab Lianlian from his arms.

"Hey, hey! What's the matter with you? Not here, not now. Plus, she's just a child."

Lianlian held Jun's arm with both hands, her mouth wide open, her eyes filled with fear and confusion. She stared at her father's angry expression and didn't know what to do. She wanted to cry because her bottom hurt, but she didn't want to anger him further. Her mother's body shielding her from her father moved her to tears. She gasped for air.

Bin-Kai threw himself back into the chair. For days, despite being busy, troubled thoughts had been plaguing him, and he'd had no one to confide in, no one from whom he could seek advice.

Jun's suffering and the fact that she would likely have a permanent facial scar filled him with guilt. Just a few days of taking care of the girls made him realize and appreciate how much responsibility had been resting on Jun's shoulders. He reminded himself that he should love her more, protect her more.

He grew even more furious with his two younger brothers. They had always admired and obeyed him. He thought they had treated Jun as family and respected her. It was unfortunate that the Red Guards had attacked his parents. He understood Jun's reason for taking the girls away, and he didn't think it could justify her brutal treatment by his brothers.

Maybe there was something else? I'll find out when I see them. But now, this! I have to delay my visit until we find out Shanshan's condition. Will she live? Will this leave a permanent scar on her face? What can I tell my folks about Shanshan? She is the center of their world. They'll condemn me for neglect. They may blame me for many other things that have happened.

Bin-Kai was a perfect firstborn who'd always brought pride to his parents. Nicknamed Prince by his colleagues, he was handsome by any standard. He stood out in any crowd with his 183-cm or 6-foot-tall frame. When he got into the best university, it proved he was more than just eye candy, and his achievements and the admiration of others made him a very proud man. He tried to set a good example for his brothers to respect and love their parents, who'd sacrificed for them when their four sons were young.

The whole family had depended on Mr. Zhou's income from working in the flour processing factory he had founded, but the government absorbed it. The income became insufficient for supporting Bin-Kai, Bin-Long, Bin-Nan, and Bin-Pei. At that point, two were attending college and two were teenagers. Mrs. Zhou, who had never held a job, had to find work to earn money. Her three-inch-bound feet made her job at a factory unbearable.

Bin-Kai's parents were not fond of Jun when they first met her. They had planned to have Bin-Kai marry a traditional woman who would live with them, as was typical for firstborn sons' wives. Jun had lost her parents at a young age and had no family experience. She lacked traditional family values because she was an independent career woman.

Bin-Kai married Jun after finding out she was pregnant with Lianlian. He loved her and had planned to change his parents' minds eventually—her pregnancy just moved the timeline up for the marriage.

Bin-Kai thought Jun had won his folks over by being a caring mother for the two girls and often visiting them after the girls were in their care. His parents did them a huge favor by taking in Shanshan soon after birth. Then poor Shanshan almost died from meningitis, dragging the grandparents to hell and back again. They took Lianlian in too, to further ease Jun's workload.

Bin-Kai recalled his father's advice from the early days of his marriage.

"Make sure you can control your wife. It is good that she earns a salary. But she is a woman, and she should obey her man and his family."

Bin-Kai said with confidence, "Yes, Ba. I will. Don't worry."

No matter the reason for the circumstances, Bin-Kai felt a sense of humiliation that he hadn't controlled his wife. To be fair, though, he didn't even know what had been happening to everyone involved. He needed to know how his parents were doing. Most importantly, he had to figure out where his family stood with Jun and the girls.

The girls!

Bin-Kai raised his head and looked at Lianlian with guilt.

I should not have lost my temper with Lianlian. Indeed, she is still a baby herself.

But as a proud man, he did not say or do anything to make up for his misbehavior toward Lianlian. He closed his eyes and let out a long exhale.

Lianlian stopped sobbing. She didn't dare look at him anymore. Hiding behind her mother, she scanned Shanshan again. Meimei's head looked tiny because the white gauze covered her hair. Just then, Shanshan woke up and reached out her hand to Lianlian as if to say, "I'm fine."

Something stirred inside Lianlian. She forgot her father had yelled at her and spanked her bottom. She stared at Shanshan's tiny, vulnerable figure. Words slipped out of her mouth.

"No, you're not fine. I'm your big sister. I will protect and take care of you."

Shanshan survived, with no scars to remember the incident by.

Lianlian engraved the promise she'd made to Shanshan into her heart.

4

FOOD, CLOTHES, AND SHOES

Jun brought home food from the institute's canteen, which allocated portions according to the number of people at home — in their case, one adult and two children (Bin-Kai was away on a remote project).

All employees and their families relied on the canteen. The government encouraged citizens to donate metals, including cooking pots, as materials for construction or weapons.

Shanshan pressed her tummy. "Mama, I'm hungry."

"This is what we get for today. Have this fresh corn bun."

Jun split one bun in half and put a piece in each girl's hands. She opened a bowl and picked up a hard piece from yesterday.

Shanshan pushed the food away. "I don't want to eat it. I can't swallow. It hurts my throat."

Lianlian echoed, "I don't want it either. It hurts my mouth when I chew and swallow."

Corn was easy to grow in poor soil and a cool climate, so it was the major crop in the region. People processed it into flour and then cooked it in various forms. They used a large steamer with multiple tiers to cook multiple buns at once. They cooked corn flour by

25

shaping it into pancakes and sticking them onto the inside wall of a large cooking pot. Another popular way of cooking corn flour was to make noodles out of it. Regardless, the texture of the cornbread was very rough. The corn skins stuck inside one's mouth after chewing and swallowing.

Jun sighed. She didn't want it either. But it could be worse.

"These corn buns are better than the husk buns."

People did not waste any nutritional resources. Wheat husks became food. Buns made from them were a formidable dark color compared with cornbread's light-yellow color. They didn't smell edible. When chewing them, one felt countless little blades cutting through the mouth and throat.

Jun reminded the girls, "We're fortunate that we at least have enough corn and husk buns to fill our stomachs. The neighbors have to drink weed soup to ease their hunger."

The government controlled all resources under its planned economy. It issued time-sensitive allowance tickets for necessities such as cotton, yarn, coal, and food. People could only buy rice, wheat flour, cornmeal, tofu, cooking oil, sugar, eggs, meat, vegetables, fruits, and holiday specialties with tickets.

A child's portion was smaller than an adult's. A ticket had different expiration dates—they might last for one month, a few months, or one year. Access to necessities was impossible without the correct tickets, even with abundant money. And without proof of citizenship — a document called Hukou — people could get no tickets, thus no means to live.

Most households had to make their clothes and shoes. Many women had learned such domestic skills. Jun remembered how proud she was when she sewed a shirt for her father that made him so happy. She had made clothes, shoes, and bedding for herself and her younger sister, and now did the same for her young family. In her young family, she used their allowance tickets to buy fabric, cotton, and yarn. She knitted sweaters for everyone. After they'd worn them for a while, she'd unthread them and mix up the yarn to knit new sweaters that would better fit the girls' ever-growing bodies.

Once, Jun bought fabrics to make shirts for the girls. She got two colors of the same flowery cloth: one pink and one yellow.

"Who wants which color?" asked Jun.

"I want yellow! It's brighter!" Shanshan was excited.

"I'm fine with pink," said Lianlian.

"No, I want pink," said Shanshan.

"Are you sure? Yours will be smaller, so you must wear yours."

"I'm sure. Pink is better for me and yellow is better for Jiejie," said Shanshan.

Three weeks later, the shirts were ready. Jun put them on the girls. Shanshan's eyes became watery.

"I want the yellow one. It looks better."

"Pink looks good on you." Jun patted her head and turned her around in front of a mirror.

"But I want what Jiejie has." Shanshan cried.

"Well, from now on, you'll wear the same clothes and shoes. It costs less anyway to buy the same fabric and make two pieces out of it, than to buy two different materials."

Identical clothing, shoes, and haircuts rendered the girls practically twins.

It was a lengthy project to make shoes. The most time-consuming step was making the soles. Jun gathered less-worn parts from old clothes and glued them together with sticky juice made from flour. It had a delicious aroma. Once the glue dried, she made cut-outs of the girls' feet. For each cut-out, she used a bradawl to punch one hole at a time, threading through the hole with a thick thread made from the leaves of a special plant. With her left hand holding the cut-out sole steady, Jun wore an old, thick glove on her right hand, wrapped the rope around the glove, then pulled with effort. She did this until she'd threaded the whole cut-out. When she took off the glove to take a break, her swollen right hand made Lianlian sad.

She asked, "Mama, can I try?"

"You can. Here."

But Lianlian lacked the strength to use the bradawl or move the thread.

Jun fashioned the sides of shoes by layering fabric, shaping it, and adding a fabric hem. Before sewing to the bottom, she put cotton in between the layers so that the wearer's feet could stay warm in -20ºC to -30ºC (-4ºF to -22ºF) weather.

"Any ideas for the openings?" Jun asked the girls.

Lianlian shook her head. She didn't want her mother to spend more effort or money.

"Can we have a black metal buckle? Our neighbor Lili has them." Shanshan said.

The girls got their winter shoes with shiny black metal buckles.

5

DAYCARE CENTER

The institute's daycare center took in preschool children during the entire working day so that their parents could focus on work. Children played in a gated yard, recited famous Chinese poems or Chairman Mao's sayings, ate meals, and took naps.

When Lianlian had just turned four and Shanshan three, Jun dressed the girls in their finest for their first day of daycare. She wanted her daughters to look presentable.

Holding onto a fold of Jun's pants, Lianlian asked, "Mama, will Meimei and I be together at the daycare?"

Jun finished Shanshan's pigtails and said, "Not all the time. You'll eat and play together, but nap in different rooms."

Lianlian looked at Shanshan with relief, knowing she could watch over her little sister.

"Mama, when will you pick us up?" asked Lianlian again.

"It will be in the afternoon. When you get home, tell me everything that happens in the daycare."

"I will."

She would soon get in the habit of reporting to her mother everything that happened in her day.

On the first day, Lianlian and Shanshan joined a large group of children playing in the daycare's yard. They heard the "Throw the Handkerchief" song and played the game for the first time.

Throw the handkerchief!
Throw the handkerchief!
Silently place it.
No one telephones, and no one should tell.
Let's be friends.
Let's play nice.

It was a common game. A group of kids sat on the ground to form a circle. One child ran outside the circle, handkerchief in hand, while everyone else sang the song and clapped their hands. The running kid quietly placed the handkerchief behind a selected child and continued running as if nothing had happened. If the child who'd been chosen realized it before the song ended, then the running kid had to continue running around the circle to pick a new child. Otherwise, the running kid sat, and the one who'd been picked would start running with the handkerchief. The game continued until the teachers intervened.

Lianlian and Shanshan sat together. Lianlian liked the song and being part of a group. She sang loudly and clapped her hands hard. She glued her eyes to the runner, ensuring the handkerchief remained visible. Then she realized Shanshan had left the circle.

Lianlian stood up and walked around the yard. In the corner between the main building wall and the fence, she found Shanshan by herself; her back to Lianlian.

"Shanshan, Shanshan, what are you doing?"

"Look, ant!" Shanshan held one red ant and showed it to Lianlian.

"Come and play with the other kids."

"Okay."

Shanshan sat back down next to Lianlian in the circle. The game continued, and the kids sang in unison. Before long, Lianlian was chosen. She stood and picked up the handkerchief, then realized Shanshan had disappeared again.

Lianlian selected another child, finished running, and left the group to search for Shanshan. She grew worried when her mom walked into the yard.

"Mama, I lost Meimei," Lianlian cried.

"No, you didn't. She's here. I found her by herself in the corner." Teacher Ren released Shanshan to her mother.

That was the first time Shanshan had shown her solitary nature. She preferred to play either with Lianlian or by herself.

Lianlian hated nap time at the daycare center. One day, a teacher stopped by her crib.

"Shh. No shuffling around and making noises. You are keeping other kids from sleeping."

Lianlian held still until the teacher stepped away. But she soon came back.

"Didn't you hear me? Why are you moving?"

"I need to pee."

"Bad girl. Why didn't you go potty before nap time?" She frowned, then lifted Lianlian out of the crib and led her to the chamber pot in the corner.

On another day, Lianlian did not call a teacher when she needed to pee. She didn't want to be called a bad girl.

"You are such a nasty girl. You wet your crib!" that same teacher yelled at Lianlian and spanked her bottom.

"Go to the corner and face the wall!"

Lianlian learned that a nasty girl was worse than a bad girl. At least when the teacher called Lianlian a bad girl, she hadn't spanked Lianlian.

Napping became a daily struggle for Lianlian. She went potty before getting into the crib, but she still often found herself either dealing with a full, uncomfortable bladder or wetting the crib. She longed to vanish from her teachers' presence, as they were domineering and quick to anger, except Teacher Ren, who was never unkind to the students. Lianlian wished Teacher Ren were in her nap room, but Teacher Ren oversaw the room where Shanshan napped.

Lianlian's favorite time of the day was when they played in the yard. She enjoyed watching ants and found them fascinating.

"Look, these ants are so small!" Lianlian pointed out an army of ants to Shanshan. Their excitement attracted another boy and a girl.

Several steps to his left, the boy discovered a large ant colony. "And these are so big!"

"These are yellow," Shanshan exclaimed.

"These are red! But there's a black ant!" said Lianlian.

The boy yelled, "This ant is holding its food!"

"Will ants react to my shadow?" Lianlian moved her body between the ants and the sun. She was curious about what the ants might do in different situations.

"I don't think so. The ants know where their home is," the girl observed.

"If I cover the ants with dirt, what will happen?" Lianlian couldn't wait to find out.

"Try it, try it!" The kids shouted, and she threw a few handfuls of dirt at them.

The boy jumped. "Oh, this one is digging out of the dirt!"

"Have you ever eaten an ant? Do they taste good?" asked Lianlian.

"I don't think ants are edible," the girl hesitated.

Lianlian caught a big ant, held its head, and bit off its tail.

"Ah, it tastes so sour!" She spat out the ant's butt.

"Let me try it!" Shanshan got hold of a big ant, along with a bunch of dirt. She put the whole thing in her mouth.

More kids joined them, and they caught more ants and ate them.

The teachers saw the kids. "Stop that! Ants aren't edible."

The next day, the headteacher announced a new rule: No one should catch or eat ants.

Lianlian's curious mind shifted to other beings, like birds. But birds were harder to focus on than ants because she couldn't hold them in her hands.

One day, a teacher brought Lianlian to the office before pickup time. In the room were Jun, the head teacher, two other teachers, and Shanshan. Jun looked furious. Shanshan appeared red-eyed and swollen-faced. The head teacher was apologetic.

Earlier that day, Shanshan had bitten a boy's hand, which upset the teacher. She'd punished Shanshan by putting her on top of the window edge, higher than the kids, and closed the door. Shanshan jumped to the floor and flipped over every chamber pot to release the pee before making a quick escape. A large double metal gate secured the yard, yet a determined child could slip through the gap. Jun's co-worker told her she'd seen Shanshan standing under a roof by a road to avoid the rain in the middle of the afternoon.

Jun rushed to the daycare. "What if a car had hit her? Aren't you supposed to supervise the children?"

That incident was a sign of Shanshan's rebellious, naughty streak. Whenever such moments happened, Lianlian wished she could help her little sister, but she usually couldn't find a way.

Rebellious behavior was a no-no. The kids who followed orders received praise. Those who disobeyed received timeouts or physical punishment.

One morning after breakfast, the teachers pulled a group of ten students together. The headteacher stood at the front.

"Children, you are the top model students. To reward you for your respectful manner, we will take you to visit the museum today."

Lianlian belonged to the group of ten. She turned her searching head. Shanshan stood on the side, along with many other kids, who were all looking at the selected group with sad or furious faces.

Two carts, each guarded by an institute worker, waited outside the gate. Lianlian had seen such carts before but had never ridden one. The front was the same as a bicycle's front. The back was a four-wheeled cart that held an open box with benches on each side.

Each had room for three adults. A metal fence behind the bench prevented falls from the cart.

Each cart had one teacher and five children. The two young men pedaled. They passed buildings, then got on a straight, wide street that led to the museum. The two teachers led the children in reciting poems, singing songs, and playing hand games.

In between being engaged in the activities, Lianlian took in her surroundings. Along the paved and wide street stood tall poplar trees with straight trunks and leafy leaves that provided plenty of shade on hot days. The street was quiet, with occasional bikes and carts. A couple of vehicles passed, and each time, the children cheered.

A man with a hat swept the street. The oversized broom, double the man's height, swept from the street's center to its edge. He moved in rhythm, and his footsteps worked in coordination with each sweep, making it look as if he were dancing. When the carts approached, the man stepped aside, raising his hand in the air to greet them. The children cheered and waved back at the street sweeper.

"There!" one kid yelled and pointed. In the distance stood a tall white building under the blue sky. It was the tallest building Lianlian had ever seen. Something was on top of the building. "Teacher, what's that on the top?" asked Lianlian.

"That is the horse, a symbol of our region, Inner Mongolia."

As they got closer, Lianlian saw the sun made the white horse glow.

"The horse is running toward us!" said Lianlian.

The teacher smiled. "You're right. It's facing south, or southeast. Do you know where that is, kids?"

The children shook their heads.

"That's where Beijing is—Chairman Mao lives in Beijing. Long live Chairman Mao!"

The children repeated with excitement, "Long live Chairman Mao!"

Soon, carts arrived at the bottom of the entrance stairs. Lianlian looked up, stretching her neck. She couldn't see the horse from here. But she noticed the decorated yellow edges of the building, the white tiles on the walls, and many enormous windows. She saw red flags flapping high above the building.

A museum staff member led them to several large halls. Posters and paintings of Chairman Mao appeared everywhere. He was in different settings, in different clothes, and with different people.

Lianlian didn't understand the content. But she liked the colors and shapes on those displays, and her heart warmed when so many pictures of Chairman Mao met her eyes. For as long as she could recall, Chairman Mao had been a daily presence. He must be an important person.

When Jun picked up the girls that afternoon, Lianlian described the entire trip in great detail.

Jun listened with full attention. Lianlian had received recognition and special treatment. It was one of the few moments that brought happiness to her life. "Mama is proud of you."

Shanshan remained silent the whole time, with tears in her eyes. When Jun helped Shanshan take off her light jacket, Shanshan opened her mouth wide and screamed.

The daycare closed at the end of 1967, when Lianlian was still four. That saddened Lianlian. However, she was happy because it meant Teacher Ren would be an even bigger presence in her life—Teacher Ren had lost her job. Her house was a few rows behind Jun's, and Jun often asked her to look after the girls. Teacher Ren was always willing to help.

Her husband was an engineer at the institute. They spoiled their son because he was their only son, but his destructive actions—gambling, drug use, womanizing, and divorce—would break Teacher Ren and her husband's hearts decades later and cause her husband's premature death. They had denounced their daughter because she insisted on marrying a Peking opera actor, Mr. Ma. Many people considered opera actors to be a disreputable and valueless job. But both Lianlian and Shanshan liked Mr. Ma. He danced gracefully and made gymnastic moves that wowed kids and grown-ups. He was a nice family man who loved his wife and their two children. Toward the end of Teacher Ren's life, her daughter and Mr. Ma ended up taking care of her.

6

CHILDHOOD FUN

With house keys hanging around their necks, children ran free in the neighborhood during the day. As part of the institute, the huge neighborhood contained not only office buildings but also houses and an elementary school with a large playground. Everyone who lived there was associated with the institute.

Lianlian and Shanshan had plenty of time to fill during the mornings and afternoons. They had no store-bought toys and used creativity to entertain themselves.

They'd seen their mother making clothes for them and wanted to make doll clothes, even though they had no dolls and no fabric. One day, Jun brought home a new mop to replace the old one. After Jun went to work, Lianlian examined the new mop, which was a bundle of leftover and marginal cloth.

"This mop has large pieces of fabric."

"That's right. We can cut them into shapes and sew them together into shirts or pants," said Shanshan.

The girls got busy without realizing the time. Then they heard the door open. Lianlian panicked. "Oh, no. Mama is back early. Quick, put them away!" Jun had a short temper. The girls were usually cautious to avoid upsetting her. Lianlian lifted the blanket off the bed, and Shanshan hid their work-in-progress there.

After dinner, Jun asked, "This mop has many new loose ends... Did you two cut off the bigger pieces?" Shanshan snuck behind Lianlian and pushed her forward. Lianlian lowered her head and answered sheepishly.

"Yes. We made doll clothes with those pieces. But we made sure the mop still worked after the cuts."

"Oh? Show me what you've made."

Lianlian and Shanshan jumped up and showed Jun their work.

"I see. Look here. When you cut, leave room for sewing so that the cloth does not get smaller than you want. And here, this corner for the shoulder should be wider. Now, the stitches could be more even. Want to practice?"

"Yeah! Yeah!" Both girls jumped.

Jun showed, and the girls followed.

"Now, no more cutting pieces off the mop, or it'll become useless. I'll find more marginal fabric for you to practice with."

For both girls, dressmaking and sweater knitting became passionate pursuits that would last decades.

The girls loved climbing—both walls and trees. The northern border wall was higher than the height of an adult. It became their favorite wall to climb and walk on, their arms held out to the sides for balance. Once they mastered climbing and walking, they invented new challenges and excitement.

"I'm ready—jump now!" Shanshan stood on the ground a few feet away from the wall with her arms open. Lianlian jumped off the wall backward with her eyes closed. She fell right on top of Shanshan, making her fall to the ground.

"Ouch!" both yelled. Miraculously, neither of them got hurt.

It didn't take long for them to learn the special skills needed to climb trees, which they often did, hiding high amid the branches and watching passersby. They found trees with edible fruits or berries—some that thrilled their taste buds with delight, and some that made them squint their eyes and spit out what was in their mouths!

Other natural toys included small round rocks, almond hulls, brick debris (to make marks on the concrete ground), and the kneecaps of sheep. Small enough to fit in the hand, the shape of a sheep kneecap is neat, and can stand balanced on any of its four sides. The girls collected them from sheep distributed by the institute each fall as a meat supply, or from Jun's colleagues or friends.

The sisters also enjoyed "Little People's Books." These were palm-sized books for children, although many grown-ups liked them, too. Similar to comic books, they were storybooks with sequential drawings that took up most of the pages, with texts below the images. This storytelling began with simple, sparsely illustrated comic books. The addition of more drawings allowed for longer, more complex stories, including adaptations of Chinese classics. These books proved exceptionally good for children learning Chinese characters at various stages, and Chinese literature.

The girls had found the books in a box one day—Bin-Kai had forgotten to close the box during his last trip home. Jun guarded it and warned the girls, "Don't touch them until Baba says you can."

When Bin-Kai came home, Shanshan asked, "Baba, can we read your Little People's Books?"

"No. They're my collections from high school and college. They're hard to find."

Jun pointed out, "They're sitting in the box doing nothing. The girls could learn from reading them."

Bin-Kai thought for a moment. A knot of anxiety formed in his stomach about sharing his collection with his children, because he hardly ever shared anything with anyone. He looked at the girls staring at him expectantly. Guilt hit him over how little time he spent with them.

He said, "You can read them—but only if you make sure you don't damage them, or I'll take them back."

"Yeah!" Shanshan rushed into his arms. Lianlian smiled at him from a distance.

At first, the girls just looked at the drawings without paying attention to the words. Once they'd learned Chinese characters, the books provided real entertainment, since they understood the stories.

The playground provided more capabilities than running, exercising, and recess. Watching movies on the school playground captivated the girls. Two tall poles at the edge held an enormous screen. People brought their stools, chairs, or blankets to sit before the screen.

Many movies were made before and during the Cultural Revolution. People called them Red Movies since they served as propaganda tools more than entertainment. These movies told of the hardships of people's lives or of fighting in wars led by the Communist Party.

With limited entertainment, they served as a wonderful escape for most, especially the girls, whose favorite movies were ones about war that showcased the wit and guts of the characters as they fought their enemies.

The most accessible movies were based on modern operas and revolutionary ballets. Modern operas used traditional Peking opera elements to present socialist subjects and modern topics. Revolutionary ballets were ballets that told revolution stories. Both had well-composed music, songs with lyrics, and scenes with stage acts. Some of them developed into symphonies.

One common feature in these operas and ballets was the strong women protagonists and powerful women characters. It might be because Chairman Mao Zedong's wife, Jiang Qing, directed the creation of these artworks. It was one way for the Communist Party to promote its policy of state feminism, as Chairman Mao had a famous saying, "Women hold up half of the sky." Interestingly, the villains in these modern works were men.

The film format of these modern operas and ballets allowed for broad dissemination. Radios and speakers carried sections of these films farther into the countryside, the mountain areas, and the edges of the country. Their images were on everything—posters, stamps, calendars, textbooks, and even on bowls, cups, and cigarette wraps. For a while, these were the only available art forms. One could not escape them. In shops, on streets, or at schools, modern operas played on the speaker or on the radio. As a result, everyone could sing along or recite them. Lianlian and Shanshan imitated the singing and dancing whenever they got a chance.

Besides playing, the girls had household duties. When Jun was busy at work, the girls either prepared ingredients for Jun to make meals when she got home, or they'd make simple meals themselves. One day, they made noodles, mixing flour and water for the dough, rolling it flat, and cutting it into long strips. When Jun came home, the girls proudly showed their work, adding the noodles to the boiling water. To their horror, the noodles did not hold up in the boiling water.

"Did you use cold water when making the dough?"

Lianlian was sheepish. "Not cold, warm. Didn't you do that last time making dumpling skins?"

"You need warm water for dumpling skins, but cold water for noodles. You used the right amount of water for the dough. Keep trying."

Days later, they made dough with cold water for making pancakes. While the pancakes looked fine, they were hard to chew.

Jun explained. "Pancakes need hot water. Besides, you needed to add more water, so the dough won't be too dry."

And so they learned what water to use for which types of dough, depending on their purpose.

Operating a large steamer was challenging. One day, the water had all steamed out. Lianlian slid open the lid, trying to add water to the big pot. The hot steam scalded her left hand, making her drop the lid to the floor. Her fingers became fiery red, and the pain made her jump. She didn't tell her mother during dinner because she thought she'd done something wrong. She had hoped the problem would go away by itself during Jun's visit to a friend. But within a few hours, enormous blisters had developed on her three main fingers, and the burning sensation got even worse. Lianlian put her left hand in cold water to ease the pain, but it only provided short-term relief.

Jun came back and saw both girls squatting in front of the water bowl.

"Are you still playing with water? Time for bed," she said.

"Jiejie hurt her hand while using the steamer." Shanshan stood up and pointed at the bowl.

"Let me see."

Jun reached out for Lianlian's hand. The fingers had become little red balloons. Lianlian tried hard not to cry out.

"You should have been more careful."

Jun blew air onto Lianlian's fingers. It was not helpful. Without the cold water, the pain was worse. Lianlian couldn't help it; she cried out.

Jun examined the fingers. "We have to cut open the blisters and let out the liquid. That may reduce the pain." She used her sewing scissors and cut off the top skin of the three fingers. Liquid came out, along with blood. This made it hurt even more. Lianlian could not look at her hand any longer as the fingers looked dark red and horrible.

Jun found gauze and wrapped the entire hand. She gave Lianlian a pill to swallow. Lianlian didn't know how long she had been in this painful state. As soon as the pill worked, she was out.

A sobbing sound woke Lianlian. The light was still on. Jun was sitting by Lianlian's pillow and examining her wrapped hand. Lianlian closed her eyes, pretending to still be asleep. Her heart warmed at the thought—*Mama loves me.*

The scars on those three fingers became permanent.

In the early spring of 1968, many places, including the institute, were closed, or semi-closed, and no one focused on work. With the food supply running low, Jun and two neighbors grew their own food. Besides their yards, they had the right to plant a vast field. It was hard work in early spring when they dug the ground and prepared the soil. When it was time to plant the seeds, the two girls and the neighbors' children did the honor. Lianlian and Shanshan worked together. One of them put a seed in a hole, and the other watered it. They planted seeds for corn, sunflowers, and cabbage. They learned to cut a whole potato into pieces, then plant the pieces into the holes.

It was amazing to watch the seeds become seedlings, then grow into bushes or tall plants under the caregivers' careful watering, weeding, and loosening of the soil. The caregivers, Jun, the neighbors, and their children all took turns guarding the field to prevent people from stealing the produce before the harvest.

One night, the girls accompanied Jun to guard the perimeter of the field. While walking among the cornstalks and looking up at the sky, Lianlian saw a full, bright moon shining upon them. She paused, looking up at the moon, and felt a sense of peace and fulfillment. That moment would stay with her for a long time.

By fall, the sunflowers had turned into big plates of dark-colored seeds. Cutting, sun-drying, and protecting the sunflowers from birds took a long time, but the girls looked forward to the roasted seeds—a regional favorite. Jun even had a space in her teeth to fit a seed in for cracking—the sign of a lifelong sunflower seed lover.

Corn stood tall, ready to be harvested. Just one huge ear could make someone's stomach happy for a few hours. The potato plants gave signs of being ready to be pulled. The children were too small to use a shovel and could only follow the loosened dirt to find the dark-brown goods. Lianlian was sorry when the shovel cut a potato into pieces, but the potatoes were so large and buried so deep that it was unavoidable.

Cabbages grew in bundles. They didn't have the good luck the other crops had—the girls often found pieces of cabbage missing. Animals were hungry too and couldn't resist the tender leaves. They never grew cabbage again.

Both Lianlian and Shanshan developed a passion for growing vegetables.

7

CHAOS

"Baba!" Shanshan rushed into Bin-Kai's arms when he came in and put down his luggage. He arrived home in the summer of 1969. Lianlian was six and Shanshan five.

Lianlian stood still, unsure how she felt about her father's return. She cherished their current peaceful existence.

Bin-Kai turned to her with a big grin. "Lianlian, come to Baba!"

Lianlian stared at Bin-Kai and didn't move. She contemplated what she should do, and how she should feel.

Bin-Kai's smile faded. He remembered Lianlian's distance toward him, while Shanshan always readily approached him.

Oh, no! Lianlian realized she had made him unhappy.

"Baba, welcome home," Lianlian forced herself into a mild smile and took a step forward.

"Good. You speak politely. Have you started school yet?"

"Don't you remember? It's not that long ago we talked about this. She's not school-aged yet. Now, give me those dirty clothes from your bag." Jun walked between Bin-Kai and Lianlian and reached for his luggage.

The next day, a salesperson with a three-wheeled cart whistled in the neighborhood. After Shanshan begged and nagged, Bin-Kai gave Shanshan 10 cents.

"Share this with Jiejie," said Bin-Kai.

The girls rushed out. They bought a colored bouncing ball to play with the sheep's kneecaps they had collected for years. They squatted on the floor. As they threw the ball in the air, they made patterns with their kneecaps, grabbing or twisting them before catching the ball on its first bounce. It would be one of the few purchased toys they would ever have.

At dinner, Bin-Kai picked a piece of pork from the platter and put it in Shanshan's bowl. Meat was rare and available only on special occasions. Moments passed. He continued eating.

Lianlian swallowed the next mouthful of food, and her throat got tighter. She started sobbing.

Jun noticed the whole thing. "Why don't you add pork to Lianlian's bowl as well?"

Bin-Kai blinked. He then understood Lianlian's tears were because of what he both had and hadn't done. He hadn't treated the girls the same. But he disliked what Jun said, and snapped.

"Don't you tell me what to do," and continued eating.

"I won't if you do the right thing."

Bin-Kai put down his chopsticks and stared at Jun.

"What did you say?"

Jun's face wrinkled in disgust.

Lianlian wiped her eyes and said, "Some dust got into my eyes. I found a piece of meat." She used the chopsticks to reach into the platter of food.

Bin-Kai paused for a moment, then picked up the chopsticks to continue eating.

Lianlian was relieved that nothing bad had happened.

On a sunny, warm weekend day, the family of four ate lunch. A sudden stomachache sent Lianlian running toward the elementary school's restroom. The entire neighborhood shared the same public bathroom, built on the edge, far from the houses, to limit the odor's effects.

Exiting the bathroom, Lianlian collided with a neighbor's child who was learning to ride a bicycle. Every kid wanted to ride a bike. Lianlian followed with admiration and forgot about the time. When she finally ran back home, she found a war unfolding.

Shanshan hid behind the furniture, shaking and crying. Spread-out dishes cluttered the floor. Bin-Kai was beating Jun. Jun was shouting. He tried to silence her with more blows.

Lianlian rushed between them, hoping she was strong enough to break up the fight. Suddenly, a sharp pain in her vaccinated right arm overcame her. She turned her head and saw bright red blood flowing down onto the concrete floor. She noticed her father was holding scissors.

A neighbor, hearing the noise, came in and saw blood on Lianlian's arm and the floor. "Hey! Don't do this to your daughter. She's just a child," the neighbor shouted.

"It's an accident. I didn't mean to harm her," Bin-Kai protested. Upset with Jun, he'd picked up something from the counter without realizing they were Jun's sewing scissors.

Lianlian became the center of attention. The grown-ups, including both her parents and the neighbor, busied themselves finding supplies to wrap up the injury and stop the bleeding.

Lianlian stood there and wailed over the physical pain of the deep cut. The moment triggered her memory of seeing her mother brutally beaten by her uncles. She believed her father had done this to her in retaliation for her trying to stop him from beating her mother.

Shanshan cried the loudest. She stood by Lianlian and turned to her father a few times to hit him with her tiny fists.

"You hurt Jiejie! You hurt Jiejie!"

For several evenings, Shanshan helped Lianlian clean the cut and put new gauze over it. The cut left a permanent scar on Lianlian's arm—and in her heart.

Normally, Bin-Kai's stay lasted up to a week. This time, he showed no signs of leaving. The institute was going through a slow period. Most days, Bin-Kai helped Jun in the garden.

On a chilly spring day, Bin-Kai was one of the four "bad" men accosted by a large crowd, organized by the Red Guards, who wore banners on their right arms. They yelled slogans: "Overthrow the Black Gang!" "Step On Counter-Revolutionists!" "Beat Down Anti-Communist People!" A group of kids threw rocks at the four men.

Jun, Lianlian, and Shanshan were forced into the front row of the crowd. Jun held the girls' hands, her head lowered and her face burning.

Shanshan sobbed and wiped her tears on Jun's pants.

Lianlian fixed her gaze on the ground in front of her feet. She wanted to disappear.

The moment lasted forever. The shouting finally ceased; the four "bad" men were let go. Jun dragged the girls home without waiting for Bin-Kai.

Bin-Kai was furious. Why was he labeled anti-party? The four men were well-regarded top engineers at the institute. His meetings and arguments with the leaders didn't help. He recalled his father telling him the Red Guards had raided their home. None of these things made sense.

He felt awful that his family had been forced to stand at the front. The girls didn't know that their father was excellent at his job and was a star engineer. He needed to quiet his mind, so he went to the yard, hung his jacket on the fence, and dug and tilled the ground to prepare for planting.

Jun prepared to cook a simple dinner because she didn't want to show her face in the canteen. The stove malfunctioned, filling the house with smoke, so she opened the window to let out the smoke. From there, she saw Bin-Kai's back against the window. Her chest was about to explode with the rage she had been holding. She cried out involuntarily.

"Why did you bring shame to your family?"

She lifted the metal cover from the stovetop, her hand trembling. Without thinking, she threw the cover out of the window, and it hit Bin-Kai's lower back.

Bin-Kai turned. When he realized what had happened, his eyes filled with fire. He stormed into the house with a few big steps, at the same time taking off his belt. Grabbing Jun and pinning her to the kang's edge, he hit her with the belt. He was not selective with where he hit her and just hit anywhere his belt reached. Jun yelled and fought as much as she could, but she was no match for Bin-Kai's strength.

The noise attracted neighbors and passersby. Their yard was full of people. Lianlian and Shanshan were terrified. Lianlian had never seen her mother start a fight. The girls begged onlookers for help, but no one responded. They pushed through the crowd and ran for help.

Lianlian knocked on the door of an administrator at the institute.

"Please help. Help! Baba is beating Mama!"

The wife opened the door, and the administrator stood up from the dinner table. "Is it happening again?"

"Yes, Baba's using his belt to beat Mama!"

He followed Lianlian to the house. Bin-Kai stopped at the sight of him.

The administrator shook his head. "You are an intelligent man. Violence is not right."

"She started it!" Bin-Kai protested.

"And yet, you are the one holding the belt, especially in front of your daughters. And look at these people. You just showed everyone what kind of a man you are."

Bin-Kai sat on the edge of the kang and let out a long exhale.

"I'm in the wrong. It won't happen again—if she behaves."

The administrator shook his head again. "Young man, you have a lot going against you right now. Don't turn your family into your enemies."

Whenever Bin-Kai was home, Lianlian felt a chilling sense of dread. Shanshan and Lianlian held their breath and tiptoed daily. They never dared to ask him for anything.

Fortunately, Bin-Kai would leave again. Besides remote projects, he attended re-education camps for educated intellectuals, who were called Stinking Old Ninths.

Without telephones, Jun and the girls did not call him, nor did he call them. They didn't receive letters from him either. Even during the Chinese New Year, they hardly ever saw or heard from him. That didn't bother Lianlian, though. She did not miss him. Life was better without him.

8

STARTING SCHOOL

Lianlian's first big milestone came in 1970. She was to turn seven in April and begin her five-year elementary school education.

"Seven years old now! Time to go to school now!" This was one of the most cheerful refrains children heard from their parents, relatives, and friends.

Going to school was such a big "growing-up" moment for Lianlian that expecting to carry a school bag kept her sleepless for many nights.

While she was tossing and turning one night, she opened her eyes to find her mother examining her face.

"Can't sleep?" Jun whispered to Lianlian.

Lianlian smiled sheepishly.

Jun gently touched Lianlian's hair, then her forehead. "I was excited too before I started school."

"How old were you?" asked Lianlian.

"About fourteen. Your grandpa didn't let me go to school earlier. I had to help him with his store."

Lianlian's eyes were wide open. She couldn't imagine starting school at the age of almost a grown-up.

"Were you the tallest in the class?"

"Yes, almost a head taller than other kids. But I skipped a grade later, and that helped."

"What about Aunt Xia? Did she start school late, too?" Lianlian knew her mother was very close to Aunt Xia, three years younger than her. Jun had told her and Shanshan that they had become orphans and supported themselves in school after their parents died.

"She started at eight and stayed in the first grade for multiple years. Your grandpa wanted me to help her move forward."

"Didn't she like school? Did you like school?"

"Your aunt liked to play with friends. She didn't like to sit in a room for hours. But I liked learning various subjects. The things I learned were fascinating. That's how a person can better herself, through knowledge and skills. Once you get those, no one can take them away from you."

Lianlian stared at her mother. She couldn't grasp what Jun had said. However, she understood that going to school was a privilege, and she shouldn't take the opportunity for granted.

One morning in February 1970, Jun picked out the neatest among all the clothes Lianlian had, which could be counted on one hand. She braided Lianlian's pigtails instead of letting Lianlian do it as usual.

Lianlian's heart leaped in her chest. As she watched Shanshan alternate between puppy-dog eyes and green jealousy, Lianlian felt great pride in her importance—she was about to have an interview with the elementary school teachers.

A long line had formed outside the classroom. Jun greeted three of her colleagues, who had given birth to their children around the same time she had Lianlian. These four kids, one boy and three girls, literally grew up together, running around the same neighborhood.

During the interview, the two teachers smiled and nodded at Lianlian's answers.

"You're a bright girl. You'll be an outstanding student. I hope to have you in my class," said Teacher Shao warmly.

About Jun's age, Teacher Shao had a round face and fine skin. Her eyes behind a pair of clear-framed glasses showed kindness and wisdom. She had pigtails that reached just above her shoulders. Her teeth were neat and white, and they shone when she smiled. She had a magnificent smile.

Then came a long, nerve-wracking wait—a first for Lianlian.

After two weeks, the wait was over. On the wall outside the school office, an enormous sheet of paper displayed the accepted students' names in bold, black ink. That enormous sheet was called a Big Character Paper, commonly used in the early years of the Cultural Revolution to announce serious political decisions or punishments for crimes.

Lianlian did not see her name. With a pounding heart, she reviewed the list again, still unable to find it.

Jun couldn't find it either. She proceeded to the office and emerged with a red face, blood vessels bulging on her neck. She had just had a verbal fight with the school leaders.

"Let's go home."

With a shaky voice, Jun clutched Lianlian with one hand and Shanshan with the other. "We'll try again next year. We'll come back next year."

"Mama, what happened?" Lianlian couldn't hold back her tears anymore once they were home.

"The rule requires a March birthday; yours is in April."

"But Mama! I saw the names of the other three children who were born in the same month."

Jun was frustrated. "They said your father, being a member of the Inner Mongolia Black Gang, was the reason."

Lianlian knew from the radio and adult conversations that the black gang was an anti-communist party and comprised bad people. She knew her father was at a re-education camp called the Tangshan May Seventh Cadre School, doing hard physical labor.

If Baba were not a member of the black gang, the school would let me in, just like the other three kids! I wish Baba weren't my father!

The rejection was deeply shameful for Lianlian. She imagined everyone in the neighborhood was laughing at her, either loudly in her face or silently in their heads. As much as possible, she avoided meeting anyone. The two girls rarely went outside their yard. Now, Lianlian refused to leave the house. She even skipped seeing movies shown outdoors on the school's playground. If she had to go anywhere, she'd go out of her way to avoid the elementary school campus.

School started on March 1. Lianlian found the classroom recitations and playground shouts excruciating.

February 1971 came. Lianlian was almost eight, and Shanshan was six and a half.

Jun wanted both girls to go to school. She dressed the girls carefully and braided their hair neatly. Shanshan had trouble distinguishing sounds between numbers with 4 in them (e.g., 4, 14, 24, etc.) and numbers divisible by 10 (10, 20, 30, etc.). Jun asked Shanshan to review one more time, counting numbers 1 to 40, forward and backward. Lianlian corrected her a few times during the review, hoping she would do fine at the interview.

Ah, Teacher Shao! She recognized Lianlian immediately and patted her head. "I remember you are that smart girl. I don't need to ask you questions."

She turned to Shanshan, who was wearing identical clothes. "Who are you?"

"I'm Shanshan. I'm her sister."

Shanshan glanced at Lianlian, her big eyes shining with anxiety and excitement, her red face looking like an adorable apple. Shanshan was usually more carefree than her big sister, but right now, not so much. Sweat came onto her forehead, and her eyes flashed.

Teacher Shao looked back and forth between the girls twice, with that lovely smile on her face. "I can see that. How old are you now?"

"Almost seven. I'll be seven in June."

"We only accept children who are seven. Can you wait for one more year?" Teacher Shao bent toward Shanshan.

"I don't think so. I've never been away from my sister. If she's in school, I want to be in school. If you don't allow me in the classroom, I'll sing outside the windows. I'll throw rocks at the windows—you won't be able to teach," Shanshan said without a pause, a serious look on her face.

Teacher Shao laughed. "What if we don't have enough chairs?" she teased.

"I can bring a small stool and sit next to my sister," Shanshan answered without hesitation.

Teacher Shao stared at Shanshan for a few seconds. She tilted her head and asked,

"Can you count from 20 to 40?"

Shanshan did it. She made every sound clear, loud, and distinguishable. There was no confusion between the number 4 and the number 10.

"I cannot promise you will be accepted. But I'll recommend it," Teacher Shao said, and wrote something down on a piece of paper.

Lianlian's heart had been pounding quickly and unevenly the entire time. She'd had her right hand behind her back, making a fist, and she could sense the moisture in her palm. After Teacher Shao's words, Lianlian unclenched her fist, breathing deeply.

The list of accepted students came out. Lianlian was on it. Shanshan was not.

Jun visited the office again.

The school made Shanshan a temporary student. She didn't have to bring a stool from home; there would be enough chairs in the classroom. She needed to pass a first-semester exam to continue.

Both girls were in Teacher Shao's class, just as Lianlian had wished.

Shanshan passed her exam at the end of the first semester! The girls were both overjoyed when Teacher Shao said that Shanshan could continue to attend school.

One day, Jun said to Lianlian, "You're a first-grader now. Write a letter to Baba."

Lianlian stared at her mother, as if to say, "I don't want to!"

Jun softened her voice. "It's to show you're an outstanding student."

To make her proud, Lianlian wanted to make it look nice, both content-wise and writing-wise.

What to write? Should I ask how he's doing? He's more like an image than a real person. Should I report on our daily routines? Should I write about school and our field trip to the museum? Maybe I can tell him about those boys?

"You'll learn your lesson when my baba gets home," Lianlian had said to those kids who called them names and threw dirt and rocks at them on their way home from school.

Should I tell him that?

Chinese characters can be hard to write, especially for a first grader. Lianlian couldn't write many words. Fortunately, every schoolkid must have a copy of the Xinhua Dictionary, a palm-sized, thick book with the most common Chinese characters.

Lianlian followed her mom's instructions for writing the address, but she was embarrassed after finishing it—it looked so ugly and misaligned!

She was also guilty of wasting several pages of writing paper, which was difficult to get, especially the good kind. The girls typically filled every available space. Even though Lianlian practiced on both sides of a blank page, she still used several pages before finalizing the letter. She was happy when she finished the dull letter, yet she felt no pride. She didn't hear from him.

9

FIGHTING BULLIES

Lianlian and Shanshan had very few friends. They made up each other's universe, as present as each other's reflection. Countless times, Lianlian wondered what it would be like to grow up without Shanshan.

People treated Jun, Lianlian, and Shanshan as low-class because of their associations. Two damaging affiliations affected them: Bin-Kai's parents' capitalist class, and Bin-Kai as a target for political movements. Low-class people lacked worth. Anyone could step on them, and no one would show sympathy. Adults would think and behave this way, and their children would imitate them as they grew, the behavior becoming part of their very flesh and blood.

Lianlian often wished she had a big brother, whose existence alone would serve as protection.

"Hei Guo Di" (meaning the Dark Bottom of a Cooking Pot) was the nickname of a girl with dark skin whose family lived a few houses behind Lianlian's home. Her parents were working class, among the most honorable people in the neighborhood. She had one older brother and one older sister. Being the youngest of a high-honor family gave her privileges that extended beyond the boundaries of her family. Girls and boys begged to be her friends. She often acted as if she held the highest status in the entire neighborhood. It might have been her way of diminishing the perceived ugliness of her dark skin.

Although in the same first-grade class as Lianlian and Shanshan, she towered over Lianlian by a full head. She had two braided pigtails that reached her waist.

Right after a torrential rain one afternoon in the spring of 1971, water formed streams and ran down the sandy streets. Lianlian, eight, and Shanshan, seven, often used nature to entertain themselves. This day offered a wonderful opportunity to build sandcastles, soil bridges, or sand dams around the streams of water in the streets.

Hei Guo Di strolled down the street. She found the two girls kneeling on the ground, busy with their creativity. She watched with amusement for a while. Then she walked across one "bridge," using her right foot to flatten out the dirt. The bridge disappeared.

Lianlian gave her an annoyed look. Shanshan kept her head down and continued building. Between the two of them, it would take much more to provoke Shanshan than to provoke Lianlian.

Hei Guo Di smiled back at Lianlian. As she smiled, she destroyed a dam.

"What are you doing?" Lianlian kept calm.

Hei Guo Di became excited, with a mischievous look in her eyes.

"I'll let you build! I'll let you play! Here, build and play!" With that, she stepped onto all the dams, bridges, and castles.

Lianlian and Shanshan glanced at each other. Without saying a word, they hopped up at the same time. Each got hold of one of Hei Guo Di's braided pigtails and jumped up and down.

Lianlian had never heard such a scream from Hei Guo Di. Shanshan and Lianlian landed, then jumped again, circling her.

People gathered. Kids laughed out loud. A grown-up stepped in and pulled Lianlian and Shanshan away from the crying girl. As soon as she was free, Hei Guo Di sprinted toward her home. People could hear her sobs for a long while.

Hei Guo Di never did anything bad to Lianlian or Shanshan again. She bent her head down while in school, a big contrast to the nose-in-the-air posture she had displayed before this.

After that, the girls earned the nickname "the crazy twins." People in the neighborhood and school warned each other to stay away from them, and they did.

This was not the first time the girls had to fight together against bullies. Nor would it be the last.

In the summer of 1971, a distant relative of Jun's, Xuemei, had a baby. She asked Lianlian and Shanshan to help her during the "Month" (people considered the month after childbirth the most important time for the mother to recover). Xuemei had two other young girls, and her husband worked full-time. The family lived 20 minutes away by bike.

Summer in Hohhot was dry and hot. The best way for people to cope with hot summer days was to do activities around a well. People in many places got their drinking water by using a pressurized well (the water flowed by repeatedly pushing a handle). Such a well stood in the neighborhood's center, becoming a hub for activities. People did laundry, washed vegetables, or cooled off. Children ran around or played with each other while their parents did chores.

On a hot day, Xuemei's two girls and Shanshan played at the well.

A family of five sons lived in this neighborhood. Such families exerted a dominant, intimidating influence. People feared the boys might hurt them with impunity.

The fourth son, Dachao, about seven or eight, picked on Shanshan because she was a visitor and new to the neighborhood. Lianlian visited the well several times to get water for Xuemei. On each trip, she saw Dachao do something mean: throw a rock at Shanshan, push her, pull her hair, block her from getting water, or call her names.

On the fourth trip, Lianlian saw him pushing Shanshan so hard that she fell to the ground. No one did anything; a few people even laughed. That angered Lianlian. She grabbed a washboard, a piece of rectangular-shaped wood with carved grids. Without thinking, Lianlian swung it as hard as she could at Dachao.

Blood flew from Dachao's face. Lianlian had hit him right in the nose, causing it to bleed. He went still and silent for a long moment, then screamed at the top of his lungs. Lianlian threw the washboard, grabbed Shanshan's hand, ran back to Xuemei's place, and locked the gate behind them.

Soon enough, there came a loud pounding on the gate. Alongside the lots of noise, they could pick out shouts of "Open the gate!"

Xuemei got up and opened the gate. There stood the crying, bloody Dachao, accompanied by his two bigger brothers with sticks in their hands. Many neighbors surrounded them. This was a great show—some rare entertainment.

"What's going on?" Xuemei asked.

"She hit me with a washboard!" Dachao pointed at Lianlian.

"Is that true?" Xuemei turned to Lianlian.

"He hit my sister first." Lianlian stepped out from behind Xuemei. Shanshan stood behind her.

"Is that true, Dachao?" Xuemei looked at him.

Silence filled the space. Dachao's loud crying became sobbing. Xuemei looked around the neighbors and asked again: "Is that true?"

No one said anything.

Xuemei paused, then said, "So it's true. Now, everyone, go home. There's nothing to see here."

The two big brothers looked at each other, then looked at Lianlian and Dachao. Without saying a word, they turned around and walked away. One by one, the other people followed them.

"You and Shanshan must pack and go home," Xuemei said to Lianlian, though in a kind voice.

They all knew that something bad might happen to the girls at night or the next day. Everyone in the neighborhood would know why such a thing had happened, but it was likely that no one would do anything to stop or report it. With a high probability of retaliation, everyone would prioritize their own safety.

Lianlian learned: *when no one else stands up for you, you must defend yourself and your loved ones, and you might just make others fear you and leave you alone!*

10

FOSTER CARE

In the fall of 1971, Jun had an opportunity to co-lead a project to build a dam. It was in a remote place among the mountains that had no schools, stores, houses, or roads. It was so remote and insignificant that it didn't have a proper name. People referred to it as Xishanwan, meaning "valley of the west mountains." Jun had to live in tents with a group of colleagues for a year. Bin-Kai was still in an unknown place for an unknown length of time. Jun had to find a place for the two girls to stay, because her work location was not child-friendly, and there would be no school.

"I have to put you two in my second brother's home," Jun told the girls, eight and seven years old.

Jun's second older brother, Xi-Dan, lived in Weichang, Hebei province. It was a small town and had government buildings, department stores, grocery shops, restaurants, schools, and even a hospital. From Hohhot, one needed to take a train to Beijing, then transfer to a train to Chengde, Hebei, and then get on a bus for four hours to Weichang.

Jun and the girls stepped off the bus. A middle-aged woman smiled at them. Younger than Jun, a few centimeters shorter, and with darker skin, Qi had two long, thick, braided pigtails that reached her bottom.

Wow! I've seen no one with such long hair! I hope that someday I'll have such long and beautiful hair, Lianlian murmured to herself.

"Welcome! These are Yin, Xiaozi and Wawa." Qi extended a hand to point to the three children. Her other hand reached out to take a bag from Jun.

"May I take this one?" A boy shorter than Lianlian took one bag from her without looking at her.

"Yin is eight," Qi nodded at Lianlian. Lianlian learned later that Yin was four months older than her. She loosened her grip and let him have the bag.

"Hi, you!" Shanshan turned her head sideways to say hi to the girl hiding halfway behind Qi. Her baggy pants covered her toes and reached the ground.

"Get out from behind me! Take your hand out of your mouth! Say hi!" Qi said with irritation and pulled the girl to the front. That shocked Lianlian—she had considered Qi pleasant until that point.

Shanshan stepped forward and took Xiaozi's right hand. "How old are you?"

"She's six," said Qi.

"I want candies!" Wawa jumped around Jun.

"Oh, yes. Here, one for each of you." Jun came prepared. She reached inside her pocket and brought out five hard candies, one for each of the five kids.

Qi turned to Jun. "He just turned five."

The seven of them walked out of the bus station. Across the street, a gigantic billboard stood between two three-story buildings. On that board was a half-body portrait of Chairman Mao. It was the tallest portrait Lianlian had ever seen of Chairman Mao, and she had seen many of them. She had to crane her neck way back, even though they stood across the street. She stared at the portrait and felt mesmerized. Chairman Mao—depicted more realistically compared with many other portraits—was smiling, waving his right hand, and wearing a grass-green uniform with a red banner on his left arm. His hat had a bright red star on the front.

"Your brother painted that portrait," Qi said to Jun.

What?! My uncle did this! Wow! He must be so talented and so trusted by the Communist Party! He must be a famous person. Lianlian's admiration of her uncle was immediately elevated.

"This is where it happened?" asked Jun.

"Yeah. He was doing some final touches. If you look carefully, you can see a brush mark on that corner," Qi pointed at the portrait.

"Yes, I see. No one can finish it?" Jun asked again.

"No. No one has the skill, and no one dared to do it after what happened to him," Qi replied.

Lianlian listened and examined the portrait. She did not see any marks of imperfection.

"That is where we live," Qi pointed to the hill at the end of the road.

The hill was two stories higher than the street level. The stairs to the yard had 15 steps with no fence or guard. *What if someone falls off the steps?* Lianlian wondered while climbing up.

A man stood at the top of the stairs, with a bright smile on his face.

"Baba, Baba!" Wawa ran up the stairs effortlessly and embraced Xi-Dan's legs. Xi-Dan patted the top of Wawa's head, then moved aside to let the rest of them enter the yard. He didn't offer to give anyone a hand, nor did he take any bags from them.

Tall, though shorter than Bin-Kai, Xi-Dan had a straight back and wide shoulders. Like many men, he had a military-style short haircut. A skillful hairdresser with clippers could do it within 10 minutes. Lianlian learned later that Qi cut his hair, just like Jun cut the girls' hair.

Xi-Dan wore a pair of clear-framed glasses. His eyes twinkled behind the lenses when he spoke. Altogether, he had an authoritative air. Lianlian got the sense that he came from another world. *He must have read many books and had a lot of brilliant ideas. How lucky is Aunt?* She glanced at Qi. In comparison, she looked plain and less significant.

Upon further examination, Lianlian saw Uncle was wearing a special vest around his upper body on this hot summer day. She learned later that the metal vest held his upper body straight and prevented him from bending or twisting his upper body. He took off the vest only for sleep. It had been three years since he had fallen off the scaffold, doing the final touch-up of Chairman Mao's portrait. He could not walk very far and rarely left his house. His injury prevented him from working, so he took only half of his salary home.

Qi's job paid little too. The responsibility of two more children added to their financial strain. Jun agreed to offer compensation. Besides part of her salary, Jun paid extra money to exchange the

Inner Mongolia regional food allowance tickets into national tickets to use in Weichang.

Every meal became a competition. During waking hours, mealtime was the only time no one talked. There was only one dish on the small table, surrounded by seven of them. If any of them were shy or unaggressive, they'd end up with a half-empty stomach. Both Lianlian and Shanshan got into the habit of eating fast.

Lianlian and Shanshan had to transfer to the local school. The academic year started in the fall in Weichang, unlike the spring start in Hohhot. The school transfer documents showed that both Lianlian and Shanshan were in Grade One, Room Two.

"Is it possible to move Lianlian to the 2nd Grade?" Jun asked Xi-Dan. She told them the story of Lianlian's delayed school entry.

"Let's see. Yes, we can do something."

Xi-Dan scrutinized the documents. Using a blue pen to match the document, he altered Lianlian's transfer document. In the same handwriting, he changed "Grade One" to "Grade Two". The Chinese characters for one and two are just one stroke apart. Xi-Dan's tactic impressed Lianlian.

By the end of the first week, Qi told Lianlian, "You're in charge of washing the dirty clothes."

Lianlian had never done that. It had always been Jun who did the washing. Qi did not instruct her on how to do it, and Lianlian didn't ask, because she thought she knew after having watched her mother so often. She gathered the dirty clothes in a metal bowl, added water, scrubbed each item on a washboard, wrung them out, and hung them on the line. She felt proud to look at the full clothesline.

Qi came to the yard and checked two pieces. "Did you use soap?"

Oops, Lianlian had not. Embarrassed, she gathered the clothes back into the bowl and redid everything by applying soap and rubbing hard. Her hands became red and itchy by the time she finished. Washing clothes for the whole family became her responsibility. It was brutal in the winter because of the icy water.

Getting water was one of the most challenging chores, especially on winter days, which were plentiful since Weichang was in the north of China. The well was a 15-minute walk away. It was a reel well that had a small edge for people to stand and pull up the bucket by a rope that rolled on a cylinder with handles. It was so deep. Lianlian once stood on the edge and fainted at the sight of the darkness inside the well. That's when she realized she was afraid of heights! Once Qi rolled up the bucket of water, she had to pull it over to the edge and then pour water into their buckets to be carried home. During the winter, ice from the splashed water covered the edge, making standing on it difficult and dangerous.

Qi used a pole on her shoulder to carry two buckets. The two ends of the pole had metal chains to secure the buckets. She had to switch shoulders and take breaks from time to time during the walk home. Yin and Lianlian used one flat stick to carry one big bucket together on their shoulders. Since Yin was shorter, he was in the front, with Lianlian following. They had to coordinate their steps so water wouldn't spill while walking home. Climbing the 15 steps was challenging. Yin had to lower the stick to hold it in his hands so that the water bucket didn't slide toward Lianlian's end.

Once they got into the outer room, Qi lifted the lighter bucket and dumped the water into an enormous water tank, which was the height of Lianlian's waist. It could hold two trips' worth of water.

When Qi was too tired to pick up the bucket, she directed Lianlian to use a big water scoop to move water from the bucket to the tank.

The first time Lianlian saw Xi-Dan replacing the fish tank water was interesting. He put one end of a plastic tube into the tank, sucked the other end, then released it fast enough that the dirty water did not get into his mouth. The fish waste and the old water continued to flow into the water bowl. The fish flopped around in the empty tank. Then he filled the tank with fresh water from the big water tank. The fish tank required two buckets of water. Fresh water allowed visibility into the tank to see the fish. Lianlian was proud that she'd contributed to getting fresh water into the fish tank. It started to get on her nerves, though, that he replaced the water every week.

Do the fish need such frequent water changes? That's a lot of water. He didn't even thank the three of us for carrying the water home.

In winter, Lianlian grew resentful of Xi-Dan's love for the fish.

He does nothing at home, not even minor tasks, never lifting a finger to help cook, fan the fire, or clean. He doesn't show appreciation or guilt. And he's the only one who cares about those stupid fish.

One day, Qi ordered Yin to split wood in the yard. He hurt his hand and came into the house to show his mom.

Xi-Dan was organizing photos from his early years. "Look at this picture. I was crying so hard with my mouth wide open." He showed the photo to Qi, who was fixing a button on a shirt.

Xi-Dan turned around and shouted at Yin, who was extending his injured hand to his mom.

"Yin, stop it! Your sobbing sounds are annoying. Wait. We should take a picture of your open-mouthed crying so that we can show it to your future wife." With that, Xi-Dan grabbed his camera and focused the lens.

Yin stopped sobbing and looked at his father with confusion. Xi-Dan kicked Yin's rear end. "Cry hard!"

Yin cried out loud with an open mouth. Xi-Dan took the picture.

Lianlian stopped doing her homework and watched the whole thing in disbelief. *He beat Yin just to take a photo?*

The fish tank didn't last long.

One day, Qi and Xi-Dan started arguing. After shouting at each other from two rooms, Qi came into the inner room to yell at Xi-Dan. She had a knife in her hand because she was preparing dinner.

Xi-Dan jumped to his feet and pointed to Qi. "Are you threatening me with that knife?"

"What?" Qi realize she was holding the knife.

"No. I was cutting vegetables to cook. I don't have any spare time besides cooking and taking care of everyone, including you, the biggest baby."

"Who's the biggest baby? I contribute to this household!" Xi-Dan shouted.

"Yeah, with your pathetic salary and doing nothing but staring at your fish." She went to the outer room and returned with an ax. Before Xi-Dan realized what was happening, Qi smashed the tank so hard that it broke into pieces. The water splashed everywhere. The fancy, colorful fish flopped around on the ground, then grew still.

Xi-Dan grabbed Qi's long, braided pigtails and dragged her to the outer room.

Yin and Lianlian left the dinner table where they'd been doing their homework. Yin tugged hard on Xi-Dan's free arm, and Lianlian pulled Xi-Dan's hand that was holding Qi's hair. The loud crying of children filled the house.

Xi-Dan stopped. He saw Wawa cowering in the corner and released Qi. He murmured something and went back to his usual sitting place. At the bed's edge next to the window, he stared at the place the fish tank used to be.

Yin and Lianlian went to the outer room and fetched a broom and a dustpan. As they swept up the debris from the floor, they glanced at each other. Lianlian saw silent gloating in Yin's eyes and knew she wasn't the only one feeling satisfaction.

She was relieved that Xi-Dan hadn't continued with the physical violence like Bin-Kai would have. That was also the moment she realized she was on Qi's side one hundred percent. Qi was the one holding up the household, just like her mom was for her own family. Her disappointment with her uncle taught her a lesson: how a person seems on the surface could be misleading, and time will reveal their true character.

There was one thing Lianlian was not happy about with Qi. The school was forming a choir, and after auditioning everyone, they selected her to join. This meant a lot to Lianlian because she was invited to join one of the few school activities—she felt excited and proud.

Qi did not like it. Overwhelmed by five children, a sick husband who didn't help with housework, and a full-time job, Qi required

Lianlian's help with cooking, cleaning and childcare. Staying late at school to practice in the choir meant no one carried out those chores.

Qi didn't sign the consent form, so Lianlian couldn't join the choir.

Lianlian couldn't understand it. *My being selected to join the choir would thrill my mom.*

Besides needing help around the house, Qi also struggled with enough food to feed the family of seven. She brought up the matter during Jun's visits, hoping Jun would raise the allowance they had agreed upon.

Friction between Jun and Qi and Xi-Dan grew.

11

XISHANWAN

In the late spring of 1972, before school ended, Jun arranged for Lianlian and Shanshan to take a long-distance bus to join her at the Xishanwan project site. The bus made many stops along the way to drop off and pick up people. It was the only way to get closer to Jun's location, though it didn't take the girls all the way there.

The bus was full. Besides people, there were lots of bags and boxes both inside and on top of the bus. Lianlian and Shanshan did not have seats, which cost extra money. Instead, they had to sit on someone's luggage in the middle of the aisle.

Not long after the bus departed, Lianlian got seriously ill. Her stomach was turning like a wheel, and her head was hurting as if someone were squeezing it. Before she could say anything to anyone, she vomited. Fortunately, she was sitting close to the doorway and didn't mess up anyone's clothing.

The driver, a middle-aged man with a bulky body and a heavy beard, stopped the bus, cleaned the doorway, and asked loudly,

"This poor girl needs our help. Could anyone give up their front-facing seat for her?"

A young man got up and let her sit in his seat.

"Thank you," the driver waved at the volunteer. "We must look out for each other."

The eight-hour bus drive was tiring and long. From time to time, the driver stopped between two stations to let the passengers get fresh air, stretch their legs, or relieve themselves. There was not much going on along the road—no houses and no trees. Most of the time, the horizon was flat or with a curvy hill. Occasionally, they saw villages far away, with houses mostly made of dirt.

That was the first time Lianlian had seen such scenery—empty and endless, almost a wilderness.

One time, a passenger yelled, "Deer!" At once, the driver stopped the bus and ran out with a gun. Several minutes later, he came back empty-handed. "Too bad. A delicious dinner gone!"

The bus finally arrived at its destination. By that time, most passengers adored the girls, especially Shanshan, whose cheerful personality and singing voice had entertained everyone. The bus driver left the girls and their bags at the platform and drove away.

Lianlian looked around and found no people or animals. The sun was setting. The concrete platform was just a shed with a floor, one wall, and a roof. It stood as the only structure in the vicinity.

As the shadow of the platform grew longer, Lianlian grew worried. *Where's Mama? What if she doesn't come?*

Shanshan hummed and jumped. She picked up little rocks from the ground and kicked them. She concentrated on kicking the next rock farther than the earlier one. "Look! Jiejie! Look! This one is the furthest!"

Just then, Lianlian saw a cloud of dust moving toward them on the solitary dirt road. Soon, a truck stopped in front of them, and

Jun jumped out of the passenger seat. Lianlian couldn't recall a happier moment than seeing their mother.

Jun and her colleagues lived in six tents that formed a camp. The tents—one for the ladies and five for the men—were spacious. A tall man could stand up straight with no problem. And with large doors, there was no need to bend when entering. They could each easily accommodate several beds and simple furniture. Since there was no electricity, they used oil lamps.

Jun had two roommates. One childless lady worked alongside her husband, who lived in another tent with the guys. Another lady, good-looking but obsessed with cleanliness, was single, and people called her an old maid behind her back.

Jun added a folding bed for the girls to sleep on together, with their heads on opposite ends. It comforted her that the girls were here with her after eleven months with her brother's family. Even though no one knew when the project would end, she believed she could manage both the job and parenting. The girls' expressions and behavior showed they were better off here.

The camp was a big family. A cook prepared three meals a day. People used their bowls to get food during designated times, then walked back to their tents to eat. Grown-ups worked during the day. Lianlian and Shanshan filled their days with chasing butterflies, picking wildflowers, doing the schoolwork Jun had assigned to them, and bothering the chef, who didn't mind being bothered. In the evenings, people played cards, chatted with each other, or wrote letters. The single lady practiced a pear-shaped stringed instrument. Lianlian and Shanshan nagged the grown-ups for stories.

Everyone liked the girls because they brought joy, songs, and dance. They often helped the girls with their schoolwork. One guy took the girls fishing in a nearby creek. A different guy took them berry-picking. Jun's roommate's husband was handy. He made various-sized baskets from the soft branches of bushes.

"Call me Baba, and I will give these baskets to you," he teased.

"Baba!" Shanshan called out without hesitation, and she got four baskets.

Lianlian was mad at Shanshan. When they were alone, she accused her younger sister. "What are you doing? He's not our baba."

"So what? It doesn't matter what I call him. But here—we got the baskets!"

"So what? Truth should be truth!" Lianlian protested.

"I didn't change the truth. I just wanted to get the basket," said Shanshan.

There were no evil people, no bullies, and no other children to grab the spotlight from the girls. People had no worries and no fights. Life at Xishanwan was a fairy tale.

Two months after the girls arrived, the entire camp was packed up. Jun and her colleagues put fragile items inside the bedding and folded the bedding into neat and tight squares. They packed a lot of stuff into just one truck. That might be where Lianlian learned her packing knowledge and skills.

People needed to take the train to get home. Jun didn't have enough money to buy tickets for all three of them. One of her colleagues had an idea.

Jun held Lianlian's hand and gave the tickets to the conductor at the gate. "One adult and one child."

As they passed the gate, Lianlian rushed on the train and watched out of the window as Shanshan entered the gate.

The conductor grabbed Shanshan by her jacket, identical to Lianlian's. "Wait. Where's your ticket? Did I just see you a moment ago?"

Shanshan pulled her body away from the conductor. "Yes, you did. I was with my mama. I had to go out of the gate to give a letter to my uncle. Mama has my ticket."

Being hushed by other passengers, the conductor reluctantly let Shanshan pass through the gate.

Shanshan was flexible and even naughty, and Lianlian was stiff and honest. This wasn't the first time they had had to play different roles to help their mother.

12

BRAVE SHANSHAN

Like many children of their generation, Lianlian and Shanshan did not have store-bought toys. They had to be creative in repurposing household items into playthings. They were thrilled to find out they might be able to play the hottest game in town by asking their father.

The game was played with cigarette box wrapping papers. With a perfect rectangle shape after being flattened out, these papers had artistic designs, were made of high-quality materials, and could be folded into various shapes and forms. The game was to fold a wrapping paper into a triangular shape, then throw it at another one on the ground to flip and win it.

Like many men and women, Bin-Kai smoked one to two packs of cigarettes per day. Cigarettes were cheap. Non-smokers were rare, and a person might get a glare if they declined an offer of a cigarette from someone.

Bin-Kai had kept his cigarette wrapping papers, even when he was away from home—he'd save them and put them together with the ones at home. Lianlian and Shanshan saw him straightening and putting new ones into a big box that was almost full.

Shanshan dared to ask, "Baba, can I have one?"

Bin-Kai closed the box and put it inside a closet. "These are for boys. I'm saving them for your brothers."

Bin-Kai had always wanted boys to carry the family bloodline. Plus, he had grown up with three brothers, and a family without boys seemed to him to lack something.

Lianlian had often wondered when her brothers would come.

One night when Bin-Kai was at a remote site, the three of them were in bed. There was a hurried knock on the door. A lady friend of Jun's came over after being beaten by her husband. Jun sat her friend on the other side of the room to comfort her.

"Maybe I will have another child. That way, he'll treat me better," the friend said.

"Are you kidding? Having children doesn't change the way men treat us. Children are no help except to tie us down," Jun whispered.

"You have two."

"Yes, but they were both unplanned, and I discovered those pregnancies too late. I don't regret having them. But I'm careful not to have any more."

"You managed not to have any more children?"

"Shh. Don't tell anyone: I had three abortions after Shanshan—three boys. I aborted the first two without telling my husband. The last fetus died inside me after he kicked me during a fight."

Jun didn't realize Lianlian had not yet fallen asleep.

I'll never have brothers. Lianlian murmured to herself and drifted off into unconsciousness.

To Lianlian and Shanshan, there was only one possible benefit to their father being home, which was that maybe other kids would not dare to bully them. That hope quickly vanished after Bin-Kai got home. He was friendly to their neighbors, even when women said nasty things to Jun or when kids did bad things to the girls.

His fights with Jun brought more nightmares. Other children simply thought of those family conflicts as amusement, and they'd rush to watch as if a circus was in town. When they saw the girls at school or in the neighborhood, kids called them names and laughed at them because of their parents' fights.

One day, when a fight started again, Lianlian ran to seek help. But her knocks on many doors went unanswered. Her tears had soaked her sleeves. Her legs trembled like jelly. She didn't know how long it had been when she noticed the day growing darker. With nowhere left to turn for help, she dragged herself back home.

Passing through a group of bystanders, Lianlian saw the door wide open, and the light was on. There was no noise or screaming. Lianlian rushed into the house and saw two police officers in uniform, one man and one woman. Her father stood by the door to his inner room with his head lowered. Jun was lying on the kang on her side, moaning with pain. Shanshan stood by the stove, a blank expression on her face.

The man officer nodded at Lianlian and said,

"Your little sister brought us."

What! The police station was 30 minutes away! Impressed, Lianlian patted Shanshan's arm in approval.

"Examine her. See how bad the beating is," said the male officer to the female officer.

"Can we use the inner room?" asked the female officer.

Bin-Kai nodded and opened the door.

The female officer helped Jun get up and go inside the little room. Minutes later, she reported back, "Lots of marks and bruises over her entire body."

The man officer took off the handcuffs from his belt, rotated them between his hands, and said,

"We consider this a crime. If you do this again, you will go to jail."

After a pause, Bin-Kai said,

"I promise I will not beat her again."

"You will not beat her under any conditions," said the officer.

"I promise, I will not beat her under any conditions," answered Bin-Kai.

"You'd better keep your promise. You are now on our watch list."

The officer was ready to leave. He moved toward the door and stopped.

Shanshan stood on the threshold, her back against one side of the frame, and her foot blocked the door.

"Little girl, you don't want us to go? Your father promised not to hit your mom again."

"But he didn't promise not to hurt us. He's done that to my sister. I brought you here. He might beat me after you leave," said Shanshan.

The two officers turned to Bin-Kai.

"I promise I will not beat you or your sister either." Bin-Kai's voice was shaking. He had just realized how much he had traumatized his daughters.

The officer looked at Shanshan and asked, "Does that satisfy you?"

Shanshan released her foot and stepped aside from the door.

The officers left.

Bin-Kai kept his promise after the officers left. He was unhappy with himself. Even Shanshan stood up against him. He sighed. He couldn't sleep that night.

Neither could Lianlian. Her ears were alert—every tiny sound from the inner room would make her flinch. She worried something might go wrong again.

It was peaceful for several days. Lianlian and Shanshan helped their mother by bringing food from the canteen because she needed to stay in bed for two days to recover.

Bin-Kai locked his room in the morning. He returned for a nap after lunch, went to work in the afternoon, ate dinner out, and returned to sleep at home. During those few days, his strong alcohol smell was more unmistakable and disgusting.

13

MOON FESTIVAL

Bin-Kai lived at home much longer than ever before. Lian-lian never figured out why he slept in the small back room, not on the same kang as other families did. Not only that, but he put a lock on the door and left the lights off when he was out. The small room had no windows to the outside, just one window on the door, looking into the big room. With the lights off, the girls could see nothing inside the small room except the area immediately around the door. The girls were told not to enter his room, and they did not dare.

The Moon Festival was to come on August 15th of the lunar calendar. People celebrated it for a week. Since it was one of the biggest holidays in China, each citizen had extra allowance tickets.

"Did you pick up the allowance tickets for this month?" Jun asked during dinner. When Bin-Kai was not home, Jun was the one to pick up the tickets on the first day of each month.

"Yes," Bin-Kai responded, putting a bundle of noodles into his mouth.

"There should be special tickets for the Moon Festival items, such as moon cakes. I heard there were tickets for grapes and sour apples. Anything else?" asked Jun.

A mooncake was a labor-intensive, fancy baked good specially made for the Moon Festival.

The girls grinned at each other. There were no black markets or free markets. Even if someone had money, there was nowhere to buy mooncakes. But they could have mooncakes during some holidays, like the Moon Festival.

"Extra cooking oil and pork," said her father, finishing up his last mouthful of noodles.

"Will you let us use the tickets?" asked Jun.

"We'll see. For now, I'm holding onto them," said Bin-Kai, putting down his bowl and chopsticks, and leaving the table to get a toothpick.

"Just get the food before the holiday, in case they're short of supply," said Jun.

"Of course," said Bin-Kai, with impatience.

It was quiet for days after that. In the mornings, Bin-Kai would lock his room before getting breakfast at a diner. After eating, he'd go to work, then return for lunch and a nap. He'd work more, eat dinner, and stay in his room with the door closed all evening. He hardly said a word to Jun or the girls.

Lianlian and Shanshan tiptoed whenever Bin-Kai was home.

"One of my classmates had half of a moon cake in school today," Shanshan told Lianlian after they got home from school.

"They were showing off. I wonder when Baba will get our moon cakes?" Lianlian asked.

"And other good stuff." Shanshan made a loud gulping noise. Lianlian poked her arm and laughed.

Another day passed. They watched Bin-Kai go in and out of the house. He still didn't say a word to them.

"Did you see Baba coming in with a big bag before lunch?" Shanshan asked Lianlian in an excited voice.

"Yes," Lianlian nodded, her mouth watering.

"What could that be?" Shanshan put her hands around her face and searched the dark inner room as best as she could through the window.

"Hopefully, he'll tell us at dinner," Lianlian said.

At the dinner table, Shanshan tried to say something to him, but his expression was too intimidating. Even though she was closer to him than Lianlian was, she had learned to keep her mouth shut and behave carefully when he looked like that. Plus, he'd been distant from her ever since she had brought the police home.

Jun broke the silence.

"Did you get the festival treats?"

"Yes, I did," said Bin-Kai in a calm tone.

"Well, where are they? The girls have been waiting for them," said Jun.

"Don't you tell me, 'girls this, girls that,' using the girls to control me?" Bin-Kai's tone stayed calm. "I decide when or whether to bring the treats out of my room. I'm the head of this household."

A chill ran down Lianlian's spine. She froze, chopsticks in hand, wondering what she should do. She knew one more word from her mother would trigger a change of tone in her father's voice, and then a fight.

Jun remained silent. She looked at the girls, then continued eating. Nothing happened that evening.

In the following days, the first thing the girls did after coming back from school was to peek through the window into the small room. They saw changes on the tabletop. There was wrapping paper one day. There was a box the other day. They waited and waited to hear their father announce good news at dinnertime or bring out goodies—they knew he had the goodies and was keeping them in his room.

One afternoon, before Bin-Kai got home, Shanshan pressed her nose up to the window. "I think those are grapes in the middle of the table," Shanshan said and kept her hands around her face.

Lianlian pushed her to the side. "Let me see. Yes, they are. Wait a minute, are they going bad?"

Shanshan put her head next to Lianlian. "Yeah, they are. Look on the right side—wild apples! I think we only had those once."

"Right. Two years ago? They were much more sour than regular apples." Lianlian swallowed.

"That's right. They're sour apples," Said Shanshan.

"Where are the moon cakes?" Lianlian's eyes searched the dark room.

"Maybe in the box? That's a nice box. I love the picture on the side," said Shanshan.

"I hope he'll let us keep the box to play with." Lianlian liked containers, no matter their shape or material.

More days passed. No word from Bin-Kai. It was as if this were a regular month with nothing special going on.

"Look! The table is clean!" Shanshan raised her voice, pressing her nose on the glass.

Lianlian looked into the inner room. There were no signs of food or goodies. She looked at Shanshan in disbelief. The corners of Shanshan's mouth sank lower; her eyes filled with tears. There was a big lump in Lianlian's throat, too. She swallowed hard to push back her tears.

It was the only Moon Festival they'd ever spent with their father. It was the worst.

They never figured out what happened to the goodies, especially the mooncakes.

14

DIVORCE

A harsh and familiar siren interrupted the classrooms.

"Children. Leave your books on the tables. Now, line up and run to the tunnels!" said the teachers.

Lianlian lined up with her classmates outside the door. In an orderly fashion, they ran to the playground filled with tiny caves and tunnels that were the height of an adult. Inside, the kids sat on the ground in groups.

The early 1970s were a time when nuclear weapons were a huge global threat. Radio shows, newspapers, and public posters all talked about how nuclear weapons could release harmful radiation. To prepare for such a disaster, people dug tunnels and hideaways underground.

Inner Mongolia had strategic importance given its proximity to Mongolia, a country occupied by the Soviet Union. That put the autonomous region on high alert for air defense. The provincial government established the defense department of the region and recruited talent.

That summer, Jun applied to the defense department and became the chief engineer in charge of provincial defense planning, preparation, and maintenance.

This was a huge undertaking, and it only happened after a long period of self-debating. Jun had hated working in the same place as Bin-Kai. His dreadful political reputation made her ashamed and disrespected. Because she cared deeply about her reputation and recognition, she felt self-conscious when people stared at her black eyes or facial bruises. She resented not being selected for important projects or receiving appreciation for her hard work and contributions. She had been feeling suffocated for years.

In this new job, Jun was the only person in charge of an important department. She authorized funding and assigned people to various projects. Her office was enormous. She often held meetings there with many attendees.

Bin-Kai didn't express his opinion of Jun's new job. But he was furious that Jun hadn't even discussed the matter with him. To be fair, though, he knew if she had, he would have disagreed, and he knew she knew that. He admitted he should be proud of her. But he sensed a threat — that she was in charge of the entire defense department of the provincial government. She had been strong-headed and hard to control, and this new position might empower her even more. *How did she get chosen? Is she that good?* He asked himself many times.

Whenever he was at home and working on local projects, he'd keep up his usual behavior—rarely grinning, seldom speaking with his family, living in the inner room and locking his door when he was out.

Jun and the girls continued walking on eggshells—and peeking into his room through the window in the door when Bin-Kai wasn't at home.

"Did you see the knives by his pillow?" Lianlian stared through the window.

"Yes. Maybe for building his birdhouse?" Shanshan pointed to the pieces on his desk.

"Not sure. He may need sandpaper or a small saw for that, but not knives. Plus, why are they by the pillow and not on the desk?" Lianlian questioned.

They told Jun what they'd seen.

Jun peeked into the room. Her face became pale. She turned to the girls and said, "They're daggers."

Few people owned guns or other weapons. Daggers were the most dangerous weapons and were associated with killing people.

Shanshan's puzzled face mirrored Lianlian's confusion.

"Is he fighting bad people who might come to hurt him or kill him at night?" Lianlian asked. People often referred to criminals who were violent, rough, young, and strong as "bad people."

"Is that why he has the daggers—for self-defense?" asked Shanshan.

"If so, that would be dangerous. He sleeps inside the little room. Whoever tries to kill him will have to go past us first," Jun said.

"So, we might be in danger too," Lianlian murmured.

"Can we ask him about the daggers?" asked Shanshan.

Jun looked at Shanshan, thinking. Then she said, "You ask him when he's in a good mood. He likes you, so he may not mind."

Shanshan nodded with an air of excitement. It was as if she'd gotten the most important assignment in the world.

Two days later, when Bin-Kai was out for breakfast, Shanshan told Jun and Lianlian, "Baba said those daggers were for anyone who might hurt him, not just for bad people."

For many nights, Lianlian could hear her mom turning restlessly, and sometimes sighing or taking deep breaths.

One day, the girls had just put the lunch on the table when Jun and Bin-Kai came back from work.

Bin-Kai stormed in with heavy steps. Something had bothered him for weeks. The girls' unfriendly attitude contributed to his unhappiness at home. Jun's new job and her authority at work reminded him of his situation. He had always been proud of his work. But even work made him feel uneasy, especially when one of his teammates underperformed and the head blamed him for the quality of the project under his supervision.

Without a word, Bin-Kai sat at the dining table and picked up his chopsticks. Jun and the girls sat too and quietly ate. Lianlian could sense that something wasn't right. She struggled to draw each breath in the stifling air. Her stomach started to turn and swirl.

"My tummy hurts. I'm going to lie in bed," she said, putting down her chopsticks and bowl. This was not the first time her tummy had hurt, and if she lay flat on her stomach, the ache would go away.

"No. You stay at the table and finish your lunch!" Bin-Kai said in a deep voice.

Lianlian froze there, with her hands on her tummy, tears in her eyes.

"She's hurting. Let her rest," said Jun.

"It's your fault. You've spoiled them and now they have no manners!" said Bin-Kai.

There was silence. The only sounds were Bin-Kai's chewing and his chopsticks touching the bowl.

"You lie down and rest," Jun nodded at Lianlian.

Bin-Kai put his bowl down with force and pointed the chopsticks at Jun.

"How dare you go against me?"

There was a fire in his eyes. The corners of his mouth lowered, meaning he might have decided something.

Lianlian was alarmed—her stomachache disappearing because something more frightening occupied her mind. Jun didn't say a word. She stood, tapped Lianlian's head, then Shanshan's. They both stood. The three of them walked out of the house without saying a word. They left everything.

Jun's new office became their shelter. She introduced the girls to her boss. "My daughters, Zhou Lianlian and Zhou Shanshan."

The formal introduction made both girls feel a sense of being grown-ups and of being important. The girls glanced at each other, and both realized they should now be more mature and accountable.

Jun's boss ordered two temporary folding beds and bedding for them. Lianlian and Shanshan shared one bed.

Jun filed for divorce, which was a foreign notion to many Chinese. Jun cited her fear for their lives. She stated Bin-Kai's history of domestic violence, recent actions against his family, and his keeping of daggers. When the judge asked Bin-Kai about the daggers, he confirmed he had them and might use them if necessary, although he didn't specify for what purposes.

Bin-Kai never believed Jun would divorce him.

Sure, our marriage may not be as good as other marriages. But a divorce? That is laughable. Is she playing a game to earn my respect or my attention? But I have to say she has been strong to raise the two girls by herself. She is very gutsy to file for divorce because being called a divorcee could bring tremendous shame, and she cares about her reputation. Am I really that awful?

Bin-Kai thought hard. He admitted to himself that he'd done things that were not commendable. For example, the daggers reflected his recent penchant for owning manly toys. A group of friends shared their passion for daggers and helped him secure two. He ordered the girls around to assert his position as head of the household. Deep inside, he wanted to connect with his children yet struggled to do so. With Jun, he knew he should have been more understanding and supportive and shown his appreciation of her carrying the household responsibilities by herself.

But a man should be a man—we don't bend, we don't compromise, and I don't apologize to my wife or my children, he concluded.

Bin-Kai laughed at Jun.

"Fine. Go ahead. I'll wait for you for three years. You'll regret it, and you'll come back to me. I can take both girls. I won't pay child support if you take them. Raising them will be expensive, which I'm sure you've considered."

Jun's salary was 37.5 yuan, and Bin-Kai's was 55 yuan. It would be tight for the three of them to live on 37.5 yuan per month.

Jun answered, "With the way you treated them, there's no way I'll let either of them live with you."

The girls were relieved at their mother's answer.

They saw Bin-Kai in court for the final hearing and decision.

Toward the end, Shanshan asked, "Can we have the Little People's Books? We love them, and you don't read them anymore."

Bin-Kai looked at her. "Those are my collections. I'll lend them to you to read if we live in the same house. But they stay in my collection."

Shanshan cried out.

Lianlian asked, "Can we have the two goldfish back? We got them from my uncle's house when we visited him two years ago. They're not yours."

Words squeezed out of Bin-Kai's teeth. "They're staying in the house."

At that moment, Lianlian hated him beyond what any words could express. She was so glad she wouldn't have to worry about him anymore.

Shanshan shouted back at Bin-Kai, "Go live with those bitches of yours!" They'd heard rumors he'd had affairs with a couple of ladies with terrible reputations.

Lianlian never knew what Bin-Kai did with their belongings—clothing, books, or their collection of handmade toys. They might not have been worth any money, but they meant so much to them.

PART II

FAMILY OF THREE. 1973-1977

15

JUN'S WORKPLACE

Their new life was exciting. Jun and the girls lived in Jun's office temporarily while they waited for their new house to be ready.

There was no school during the summer. Lianlian and Shanshan, ages ten and nine, spent their time under the sun and wandering around every part of the compound where Jun's office was located.

The provincial government compound had two wide gates, one in the front and one in the back. Uniformed and armed guards stood by the gates 24/7. The gates were closed with metal-fenced doors unless a car was to go by. Those on foot or on bicycles went through a small side door. To enter, they either showed their special ID cards to the guards or called their contact from the room by the gate to come and get them.

Inside, immediately after the front gate, was an oval-shaped landscape boasting a fountain in the middle. It sprayed water into the air, as high as the main building. Flowers were everywhere, around the fountain and on many sidewalks.

The main building was five stories high and spread out into two giant wings. Its roof had artistic decorative designs in red, gold, and green.

Over ten monument buildings spread out along a central line where the main building stood. Among these buildings were abundant spaces with roads, tall trees, and flower beds.

As the only children living in the compound, they visited the canteen several times a day to get meals and became acquainted with the cooks and the workers there. They teased the guards at the two gates, who invited them to play games.

There was a vegetable garden in front of the two rows of flat buildings where the fifteen guards lived. They had their own kitchen and dining hall. In their early 20s, most of the guards had various accents and came from families who lived in the countryside. The girls visited them daily and played soccer, basketball, and ping-pong with them. They harvested the garden's vegetables and ate them in the guards' kitchen.

Once, a guard's shirt lost a button. Lianlian sewed it back on after seeing him struggle with the needle. Jun taught her more hand-sewing techniques to make sure that the stitches were the same size and stayed in a straight line. Lianlian applied her new skills to fix more shirts and pants for the guards, who always welcomed the girls with big smiles and warm greetings.

The girls interacted with other grown-ups, including Jun's colleagues, workers on various construction projects, and people who visited for personal reasons.

Once, a group of workers set up a platform to prepare construction materials to fix a spot behind Jun's office building. They had to cut a large, flat, metal plate into various shapes. A worker wore thick coveralls that covered his arms, legs, and even his shoes. He put a protective helmet on his head, which had a rectangular window made of dark glass. He used both hands to hold a long tube that had a head at one end. Once the power was on, an orange and blue flame came out, forming a narrow beam of fire. The worker moved the beam to follow the cut marks on the plate. A piece of shaped metal came out. The process fascinated Lianlian. She sweet-talked the worker into letting her try it. After some hesitation, he agreed.

"Here, you hold the handle of this thing," he showed Lianlian. "Let's call it the firegun. Make sure both hands coordinate in this way to balance the weight."

Her first try yielded a small piece with zigzag edges. She changed her grip and figured out how to keep her hands steady. The next piece was rectangular. She moved slowly and steadily with her hand and finished tracking the marks before her hands even got tired. Turning off the power, she asked, "How did I do?"

The worker examined the piece and said, "You did a great job! We can use this piece. Hey, quick learner, want to be my student?"

Lianlian was proud and thought that if she couldn't get a job in the future, she could work cutting metal plates!

"Not bad for a young girl," a low voice came from behind her.

Lianlian turned. She had seen this fellow a few times now. He often wandered around the main building, watching the workers and the girls from a distance.

"You can call me Uncle Wei. Glad to meet you two," he nodded to Shanshan and Lianlian with a sincere smile.

Later, the girls learned Uncle Wei had filed a complaint against his ex-employer for mistreatment and had to constantly return to the provincial capital to check on the status of the complaint process. Every time he visited the main building, he came over to have a conversation with the girls, and sometimes Jun. Gradually, the girls got to know him very well. His wife had left him and taken their son with her. He had no family anymore. Tall and well-built, he didn't have the scholarly air that Bin-Kai and Uncle Xi-Dan had. That made Lianlian wonder if he made a living with his hands, not his head. He was gentle and warm. The only thing Lianlian felt uneasy about was his gold tooth. It showed when he laughed, which didn't happen often. From the movies and Little People's Books, she'd learned that only bad people—like gangsters—had gold teeth.

16

NEW HOME

The new house Jun and the girls moved to was in one of the provincial government's many residential neighborhoods. This new neighborhood was small and had only four one-story buildings in two rows. Each building had eight apartments. Builders constructed them so that one unit had 1+1/4 rooms, the next one had 1+1/2+1/4 rooms, and the rest repeated the pattern. The full room had a built-in kang that took up about 40 percent of the space in the room and was heated by the cooking stove in the kitchen—a 1/4-sized room.

The stove in the kitchen used coal and was powered by a fan in a box with a handle to pull and push. Besides the cooking stove, people also had at least one other iron stove for heating in the main room and for cooking. This freestanding stove generated heat that traveled through metal pipes around the rooms and went out through a hole in the wall or window.

A family of four or more got a (1+1/2+1/4)-sized apartment. Jun's three-member family received a (1+1/4)-sized unit in the middle of the building.

There was a strong tradition that houses should face south. Those houses that had to face other directions were less favored, even avoided. All the houses in their neighborhood had a south-facing door and one large south-facing window in the main room. The ½ room also had a south-facing window. All kitchens had a north-facing window that was much smaller and high above the ground—the girls had to step on a chair to open or close it. It provided enough daylight for the kitchen.

In Jun's main room, the west side had a desk with two chairs beside it. On the eastern wall sat the iron stove next to the door to the kitchen. The north held the wall-to-wall kang. Two wooden chests at the foot of the kang were for storing bedding and clothing.

In the kitchen, Jun put up some shelves for storage along the north wall. Having running water—albeit only at certain times of the day—was an enormous improvement over their old house. The water pipe, shared with their next-door neighbor, was on the east side, and an enormous water tank stood in the corner. They also had a wooden stand to hold a washbasin for cleaning their hands and faces.

Every home had four other important components: a side house, an underground cellar, a yard, and a gate.

The most important was the side house, called the "Cool Room." It was like a shed and not permitted to be taller than the main house. Most were tall enough for grownups to stand straight to reach the top of the structure. During the summer, cool rooms served as a storage area, a kitchen, or even a living space. Because of the setup of the buildings and the neighborhood, the side houses faced the main houses and formed part of the yards' borders.

People molded mud bricks to construct side houses. Real bricks would need to be burned in a special oven and would cost money, so mud bricks were the most economical solution for most families. It took hard labor to produce mud bricks in an open space and then dry them in the sun.

For several weeks, Jun, Uncle Wei, and two of Jun's colleagues made mud bricks in the wide-open area behind her office building. Uncle Wei was there almost all the time, and then Jun and her colleagues would join him after work. Lianlian and Shanshan jumped around and helped in any way they could.

After spreading dry sand on the surfaces of a mold, which was a one-foot by half-foot by half-foot sized wooden container with one side open, Uncle Wei shoveled squishy mud into it. Then he used a metal tool to get rid of extra mud and make the open side flat and smooth. Next, he'd turn this container upside down so that the mud came out in the shape of a brick. Once dried, it turned into a mud brick.

"Girls, do you think you can lift that?" Uncle Wei teased, pointing at the filled container.

Lianlian opened her arms, put her hands on the handles, and gave it everything she had. It stayed on the ground without even the slightest movement.

"You'll need to be several years older before you can do that," laughed Uncle Wei.

He stood with his feet apart, took a deep breath, and lifted the container, turning it over onto a patch of sand. Then, he carefully lifted the container off.

"Damn. Not smooth enough," Uncle Wei examined the results. It shifted a bit to one side.

He gathered the mud material and dumped it onto the gigantic pile, starting all over again.

Jun helped sand the surfaces of the containers because Uncle Wei refused to let her lift the filled container. "Too heavy for a lady and not good for your body."

Other colleagues helped periodically. Uncle Wei oversaw the work with a cigarette hanging from the corner of his mouth.

As the days went by, an army of mud bricks neatly lined up. As was typical in the summer, it did not rain.

Five young men plus Uncle Wei worked two full days to build the side house. After the walls and roof were built, the men covered the mud bricks with a mixture of mud and hay. This smoothed the surface and protected the structure from weather like snow, rain, and wind.

Jun designed the side house herself, which was a piece of cake for her. She made the ceiling tall enough for her to reach without a footstool. She added a built-in cooking stove, lots of shelves for storage, and room for parking bicycles and other large items. In one corner, a small, fenced-in area stored coal and allowed them to break large pieces into small ones when they needed to use the coal. Employers distributed the coal once annually, and it had to last the entire year. Some neighbors stored coal in their yards but needed to put a cover over it so that exposure didn't lower its effectiveness.

The side house's roof was slightly tilted to prevent snow or ice buildup. It also provided a surface for drying leftover cabbage leaves, which the girls would feed their chickens in winter. They'd need a ladder to climb up to the roof. Besides moving vegetables up there and getting them down after they dried, the girls also climbed up there just because—it was a place for them to rest or have a change of scenery, although all they could see from there were the neighbors' yards or other side houses' roofs.

The second most important component was an underground cellar in the yard, which served as a storage room during winter. A sizable space was dug into the ground, to the depth of an adult. The four sides and the top were secured with strong materials, except for a special opening. Finally, dirt was put on top, making it part of the yard. Without refrigerators, such underground storage rooms were in use for more than half of the year to store vegetables. Jun and the girls kept potatoes, carrots, and cabbage on small shelves. People didn't buy their vegetables at the market in the winter; instead, the institute distributed most of these vegetables in the fall, with a truck making door-to-door deliveries.

After school on winter days, Lianlian and Shanshan played rock-paper-scissors to see who would fetch items from the cellar. Lianlian often lost.

She put on a heavy hat to cover both ears and neck, a winter coat buttoned up tightly, and her thickest mittens. The opening of the cellar was above ground level. It took some effort to open the heavy cover because icicles had glued it to the frame of the opening. Careful to avoid the slippery edges, Lianlian stretched one foot down to land on a narrow ladder. Shanshan stood by the entrance, holding a basket and a flashlight. Icicles caught on Lianlian's sleeves and pants—and would have trickled down her neck if she hadn't worn the heavy hat. Before she completely disappeared from the opening, she reached out to get the flashlight from Shanshan. A few more steps down the ladder led to the bottom of the cellar. Above, Shanshan let go of the basket but held tight onto a rope that was tied to it.

Lianlian put a few potatoes and two carrots into the basket. With a thick mitten, she dug up two watermelon radishes from underneath the sand and put them in the basket. They were light green outside and pink inside—pretty and delicious. When the mitten did not work well, she had to use her bare hands to dig. After digging, she made sure sand covered the rest of the radishes.

Carrying the basket to the ladder, Lianlian told Shanshan, "Pull up now."

After that, Shanshan sent the basket back down with a water bottle. Lianlian dashed a few drops onto the sand that covered the radishes. This prevented water from evaporating so that the radishes stayed watery and crispy throughout the season.

Carrying a big cabbage was challenging. With one hand holding the flashlight, Lianlian's other hand was not big enough to hold the cabbage. Sometimes, the basket was not big enough either, especially for long cabbages. Lianlian used both hands to raise the cabbage to the ladder, then Shanshan would get hold of it from the opening. After Lianlian climbed up, she put the lid back securely.

The yard was important for storing large items or for raising chickens. The limited space between the public pathway and the main house, and between the two neighbors' yards, constrained their yard. Jun used mud bricks to build two walls, about the height of Lianlian's shoulder, to act as fences dividing their yards from the two neighbors.

Jun wanted to build a coop in the yard so that they could raise chickens and have fresh eggs. That left only a little free space for the yard.

The last component was a gate, which was a requirement for every house. Jun and her helpers made a wooden frame with irregular wooden boards they had gathered from various places. One could see through the gaps in the gate, and a small opening allowed a hand to reach inside to open or lock it.

The new house provided more stability and peace for the family of three than any other they could remember.

As fall began, the weather became more comfortable.

One evening after dinner, Jun said to the girls, "Let's have a walk along the back of the neighborhood."

She put on a long dark green skirt and a white short-sleeved top. There was a peaceful, relaxed, and confident expression on her face.

Lianlian remembered that outfit from when she'd been very young and their mom used to take the two of them for evening walks. Looking at her mom now, she couldn't help but gush about how beautiful Mom was. She hadn't seen this side of her mother for a long time.

17

NEW ELEMENTARY SCHOOL

Along with moving to the new house, the girls transferred to a new school, Xinhua Elementary School, to finish their five-year elementary education. Children attended nearby schools based on their home locations. Lianlian was a fourth grader, and Shanshan was in third grade. Most people knew the children's parents were divorced.

Lianlian had no trouble at school. She absorbed the material easily and performed well on her homework and exams. She was popular among her classmates because of her skills, fairness, and easygoing nature when playing games during recess.

Many games required no toys, equipment, or objects. Some games were short, while others could go on for some time. One popular game was "Jumping Horses," which imitated gymnastic moves. A group of any size could do this for any length of time. After playing rock-scissors-cloth, one or a few girls were selected to function as "horses." They lined up five meters from each other, their hands holding their heads and their bodies bending, so that their backs became flat and faced the sky. The rest of the girls ran toward the "horses" to jump over them by opening their legs wide and putting their hands on the horses. They continued to finish the rest of the "horses." If anyone failed or was scared, she became a horse herself.

Another was "Guarding the City." One group defended their city's gate, a square drawn on the ground. Members of the other group had to be on one foot and enter the city through the gate. When offending members fell on both feet, the two groups switched roles, and they'd keep playing. This game required balance and arm strength for wrestling.

A similar game was "Crossing the Bridge." Two lines were drawn on the ground as the edges of a bridge, which could be wide or narrow depending on the levels of the players. One group lined up on each side of the bridge, trying to prevent anyone from crossing it. Everyone had to be on one foot. If anyone lost balance to land on both feet or accidentally stepped on the bridge lines, their team lost, and the game restarted.

If the girls found soft or sandy ground, they played another game using gymnastics. They crouched down, leaning back on all fours, making tables with their stomachs facing the sky. They "walked" in that position toward a target at the fastest speed.

With a flat wall, the girls flipped toward the wall into a handstand. The goal was to see who could hold that position the longest.

The boys played different games during recess at school. One of them was "Battering Ram." One boy, holding one leg toward the knee of the other leg, bumped into other boys with the bent knee. He won if the other boys lost balance and landed on two feet.

A remarkable thing happened to Lianlian. At the midpoint of the semester, the homeroom teacher announced Lianlian's acceptance as a member of the Little Red Guards, citing her academic achievements and helpfulness. The Little Red Guards was a national political organization for elementary school children. It had many local branches, preceding the Red Guards for middle and high school students. Instead of having a red armband like the Red Guards, the Little Red Guards wore a red scarf around their necks. The school nor the organization did not give such scarves out. Parents had to prepare the red scarves for their kids.

Jun was thrilled and proud of her firstborn. Lianlian's being accepted to the political group at her age brought honor to the family. She took it as encouragement that Lianlian's future might be bright.

Jun rushed to the store to buy the bright red fabric to make a red scarf. She had once been the top officer for the Communist Youth League when she was in vocational school and at her institute. But because of her association with Bin-Kai and his family, she had never been invited to join the Communist Party, the political group that could ultimately advance one's career.

The ceremony of joining the Little Red Guards was emotional. Lianlian and three other students stood in front of Chairman Mao's portrait. A school leader tied the red scarf to her neck. The new members raised their right hands above their heads and swore an oath by repeating after the school leader.

The Little Red Guards' Choir was recruiting new members. Its practice was one of the few extracurricular activities at the school, and every little red guard wanted to join.

During music classes, the music teacher gave each kid a chance to do a solo, from the red songs or the modern Peking operas.

Lianlian was selected. But Shanshan didn't make it—she was not a member of the Little Red Guards yet, and she had trouble remembering the lyrics and very often hummed throughout a song. The choir held practice twice a week after school. Shanshan had no problem waiting for Lianlian during the entire practice so that they could walk home together.

One day after school, Shanshan declared, "Mom, Jiejie is going to be on TV!"

"Oh?! What is going on?" asked Jun.

"The music teacher said during today's practice that the choir will sing on TV. They will be recorded and broadcast!" Shanshan announced it with as much excitement as if she herself were going to be on TV.

"Wow! That's a great opportunity. Is there a need for clothing?"

Of course, there was. The music teacher asked members to wear snow-white shirts and red scarves. Those in the front row must wear black pants. Being one of the shortest members, Lianlian was in the front row.

Jun was happy to spend money to make a new shirt and a presentable pair of black pants.

To Lianlian's surprise, the TV recording provided compensation of 1.50 yuan.

This was the first time Lianlian had made any money. It was such an honorable way of bringing money to her mom to help with the household costs. Lianlian was most proud when seeing the expression on Jun's face when she handed her the money.

I want to do my best so Mom can be proud of me. I want to help her in any way I can, she told herself.

Ge Meng was a boy who shared a table with Lianlian. He lived two houses away from her.

Lianlian noticed Ge Meng first by his family name, Ge. It was an uncommon name, and Lianlian knew of only one person with that name: Ge Yanshao.

Are they related? Do they know each other? Don't be silly. There are so many unrelated people with Liu as the family name. People with common names don't have to be related to each other.

She felt she knew Ge Yanshao, Jun's first love, more than she knew her father. She had seen photos of him when Jun had visited them. Based on Jun's tone and the subtext of her descriptions of Ge Yanshao, Lianlian favored him over her father. She had figured out that her mom had left Ge Yanshao to marry her father. She wondered why he couldn't work in the same city, why she'd left him, or what had made him inferior to Bin-Kai.

I wish he were my father, Lianlian thought, more than once.

Ge Meng was a quiet boy. At the beginning, he and Lianlian didn't speak to each other. That was normal: boys and girls didn't speak to each other; it was as if they might catch a disease if they did.

On one freezing day, the stove in the classroom wasn't working. Everyone was stamping their feet and covering or rubbing their hands. Ge Meng pushed one of his thick gloves to Lianlian's side of the table without saying a word. Lianlian looked at him, and he behaved as if nothing had happened. Lianlian accepted the friendly gesture. A few minutes later, Lianlian gave the glove back to him and pointed at the one he had. He understood and exchanged the gloves so that they both alternated between the left- and right-hand gloves to warm their opposite hands.

They helped each other in other ways. Lianlian pushed sharpened pencils over the dividing line when he ran out of pencils. She let him look at her papers when he had trouble understanding the teachers' questions. They didn't talk to each other and made sure no one could see them doing any of these things.

It was different after school, when no classmates could see them. Ge Meng found reasons either to come to Lianlian's yard or to invite Lianlian to visit his home.

"My mom wants me to do laundry. I've never done it. Can you show me how?" Ge Meng spoke over the fence.

"Sure. I'll be right over after feeding the chickens," Lianlian answered.

"I want to go, too," Shanshan followed.

Ge Meng's home had 1+1/2+1/4 rooms because they had four members. His older brother was two years older. Ge Meng showed the girls his house. It felt much bigger. After looking around, Lianlian found out the reason.

"Why no kangs but wooden beds?" asked Lianlian. That was very unusual in this region because every family must have a kang. A wooden bed had a wooden board over four pillars, and its bottom was empty.

"My parents said they used to have wooden beds."

"Where did they grow up?" Lianlian felt her heart beating fast. *Is it possible they were from the same place Yanshao grew up?*

"My father was in Anhui province, and my mom was in Sichuan."

Lianlian's heart went back to a normal pace. Nope. Yanshao was born in the northeast, and those provinces are in the south. No relation. Yet, she still felt a soft heart toward Ge Meng.

"But how did your parents end up here?" asked Lianlian.

"They were placed here after graduating from the same university," said Ge Meng.

Lianlian nodded. She had heard from her mother about job placements for couples. If they wanted to be together, they would be placed in a faraway place.

She recalled her experience of not sleeping in a kang at one of Jun's remote project locations.

"It must be chilly at night without the heat under the beds."

"We use hot water bottles to warm the beds before going into them."

That must mean four such bottles, Lianlian thought. Her house had just one, and it was for healing stomach aches, not for warming the kang.

In the middle of the main room in Ge Meng's house, a big washbowl was full of water and clothes. Step by step, Lianlian showed Ge Meng what to do. With amusement, she watched Ge Meng write the steps on a piece of paper.

Another afternoon, Lianlian and Shanshan played jump rope in their yard.

"Can I join you?" Ge Meng shouted over the fence.

"Sure," answered Lianlian.

The three of them took turns jumping. It was such fun; they laughed and played until the grownups came home.

Ge Meng and Shanshan argued often.

Lianlian concluded: "A tiger and a dragon won't get along." (Ge Meng was born in the Tiger's Year, and Shanshan's birth was the Year of the Dragon).

Later, Ge Meng and Lianlian attended the same high school, but were in different classes. Upon Jun's request and Ge Meng's mother's agreement, he followed Lianlian home after night classes, for safety's sake. They hardly talked to each other at all, even when no classmates were watching. Their innocent childhood friendship had gone, and both were now shy whenever talking to the opposite gender.

18

BIG ROOSTER

Although they were always short of money, the three of them could manage with Jun's salary. She put part of her salary in a drawer for the girls to buy groceries and other necessities each month.

The girls did their bit to help as much as possible. They went to the backyard of a restaurant nearby to find partially burned coals, which were hidden in ashes and required digging. This messed up the girls' clothing, faces, hands, and arms. But they were free and made great fuel for heating the house or cooking meals.

Raising chickens was a major household chore for the girls. It was laborious, yet fun and rewarding. The girls discovered an economical way of feeding them.

When the market was open for fresh produce, Lianlian and Shanshan went to gather free vegetables daily: good ones for people to eat, and not-so-good ones for the chickens. These vegetables, such as cabbages, carrots, and celery, were leftovers, or pieces that fell off and no one wanted to buy. The girls timed it so they could gather the vegetables before they ended up in garbage bins. Then they'd put the extra cabbage leaves on the roof of the side house to dry and later bag them. In the winter, they boiled dry leaves, chopped them into small pieces, then blended them with cornmeal to feed the chickens.

In early spring, local farmers came to the neighborhood with baskets of chicks that were a couple of days old. Everyone wanted to have more hens than roosters—eggs could make up a nutrition deficit or be exchanged for other items with neighbors and friends.

One year, they had a hen named Luhua. She had feathers that blended black and white together in a very refined way, as if she were wearing a pretty dress. She was the first in her cohort to lay eggs in the middle of the summer. A few months later, she was laying two eggs, once every few days. The second egg often lacked a hard shell, so if one was not careful while gathering, it would break. Because of both her productivity and her mellow personality, the girls kept her the longest of their chickens.

Many neighbors claimed to have tricks to determine a chick's sex. Jun thought she knew such tricks, too. By the time the chickens were a few months old, people could tell a hen from a rooster. Very often, they had more roosters than they wanted.

Roosters were a waste of resources. They cost money to buy, ate more, and sounded horrible when they started crowing. They fought each other, and the fights could get bloody. Although roosters could fertilize eggs for them to be hatched into chicks, people hardly ever hatched their own chicks. Overall, roosters had little value beyond being meat. People slaughtered most young roosters for meals.

Roosters were not all the same. Jun and the girls agreed to spare one rooster. He was muscular and a winner in fights. From the very beginning, his crowing was a charming melody. When he was fully grown, his size was twice that of the biggest hen, and his multicolored feathers shone in the sun like a fancy coat. He stayed still and didn't object when the girls held him and plucked a few feathers to make shuttlecocks for kicking.

The most remarkable thing about this rooster was that he was very protective. He could tell his owners from strangers, and he considered himself a guard. He'd attack anyone he didn't know at the gate or make a loud sound to alert his owners. The girls had to hold him in their arms to let visitors pass.

One day after coming home from school, Lianlian and Shanshan attended to their chickens as usual—besides the rooster, they had five hens. Two boys who played with their next-door neighbor's son peeked into the girls' yard through the fence.

"Their mom must be such a slut," one boy commented.

"Yeah, must be such a whore if her husband doesn't want her anymore," snarled the other boy.

Lianlian didn't know what to say and didn't know what the consequences might be if she did. Shanshan said nothing, either.

Their silence must have encouraged the boys to continue. "Look at that rooster. It sleeps with five hens. What an evil example. This entire house is a prostitute garden." The boy who spoke climbed up to sit on the fence, followed by the other boy.

As they continued to badmouth the family, an angry impulse arose inside Lianlian. She picked up the thin shovel that they used to dig up chicken poop and swung it right at one boy. He was shocked and moved his body to one side to avoid the hit. His hands lost their grip on the fence, and he fell into Jun's yard.

The rooster's face turned red, and his neck straightened. He made a loud noise, jumped up with his wings wide open, and attacked the boy with his pointy beak and sharp claws.

The boy screamed, protecting his face with his arms. The other boy jumped back into the neighbor's yard, crying for help.

Lianlian and Shanshan didn't stop the rooster. They just watched, with both amazement and satisfaction.

"Stop that! Stop that!" "Get out of their yard!"

Those were the voices of grown-ups. The neighbor and the sister of the boy yelled and pounded on the gate.

Lianlian grabbed for the rooster's tail and got hold of him. Shanshan opened the gate. The boy ran as fast as he could, his face and arms covered with blood.

The boy's family came to confront Jun. Lianlian stood by her mother's side. She wanted to tell them that the boy had been saying bad things, but she didn't get the chance. Jun said one sentence that settled the whole matter: "Your boy was in my yard."

That made the rooster famous throughout the neighborhood. No one dared enter the yard while he was still living. The girls never did name him; instead, they just called him Dagongji, "Big Rooster."

19

HUANG SHUAI AND ANTI-CONFUCIUS

In 1973, when Lianlian was 10 and in the 4th grade, a significant event happened.

In the new elementary school, students had a homeroom where they stayed for the entire day except for recess or physical education classes. Each classroom had a home teacher who taught a particular subject, too. Teachers of other subjects came at a scheduled time to deliver their lessons. Each class started and ended with a loud bell. There was a 10-minute break between classes.

Each week, a group of students was on duty, arriving early to set up the stove, and ensuring it ran throughout the day by adding coal. At the end of the school day, they put it out. They also erased the blackboard after each class, cleaned the classroom after school, and did a few other chores to keep things running smoothly.

On a freezing winter morning before the class bell rang, the classroom was already full of students. Kids higher in the pecking order surrounded the stove and the warm pipes. Gao Qiang, who was the biggest bully in class despite being short and ugly, was talking loudly and laughing.

He looked around and asked, "Is everyone inside now?"

Once he got confirmation, he threatened, "Nobody leaves! And nobody tells!"

No one in his or her right mind would have dared to say or do anything against him. Once, Gao Qiang had been disrupting class during a lecture. The subject teacher had known no way to deal with him other than kicking him out of the classroom. Then the teacher asked Ge Meng, Lianlian's neighbor, to throw out Gao Qiang's school bag. Poor Ge Meng found himself caught between a rock and a hard place. He had to follow the teacher's order and gently put the bag down outside the classroom. Later, Gao Qiang beat Ge Meng in front of the entire class. Ge Meng ended up with a bloody mouth and a broken nose. He wore a nose patch for weeks. No one dared tell the homeroom teacher or the school about the beating.

After making sure everyone was inside, Gao Qiang walked to the door with a bucket of cold water. His sidekick, a tall boy, went with him. The tall boy stood on a chair after Gao Qiang nodded. He cracked the door and carefully placed the bucket on top, leaning it against the frame. Then they hurried back to their seats.

The bell rang. A middle-aged woman, the Chinese literature teacher, opened the door. The bucket immediately fell on her head, the cold water drenching her hair, face, hands, clothing, and the course materials she was holding.

Everyone was shocked, including the teacher. She stood there for a long while. Her face became pale, and her hands and body shook. She opened her mouth as if to speak, but nothing came out.

Most students were quiet, but loud laughs came from where Gao Qiang and the tall boy sat.

The teacher turned around and left. Lianlian saw tears in her eyes.

"You guys on duty, clean that up!" Gao Qiang shouted. "What are you all staring at? We're learning from our hero Huang Shuai! This Chinese literature teacher is teaching us old poems from the past. Other teachers teach us to learn and respect Confucius' ideology. They all need to be taught a lesson. They're not superior to us students! We are the new generation!"

Gao Qiang was referring to the Huang Shuai event everyone had just learned from the radio and newspapers.

In December 1973, the entire nation celebrated a 12-year-old girl, Huang Shuai, as a hero. A fifth grader in an elementary school in Beijing, she'd observed some instances in class where she disagreed with her teacher and recorded her thoughts in her diary. Diaries were homework assignments that had to be submitted. The teacher lost his temper when he saw her entries. The conflict escalated, and Huang Shuai grew helpless, anxious, and unable to concentrate on studying.

Out of desperation, Huang Shuai wrote to a newspaper to share her situation. It gained the attention of a political officer, who saw an opportunity for this situation to showcase the Anti-Confucius political campaign and education revolution. Reporters and journalists visited Huang Shuai and her school. By this time, Huang Shuai and her teacher had already reconciled and were friendly.

The People's Daily, China's top newspaper, published her diary entries and editorials from top political leaders. They also urged hundreds of thousands of young students to follow Huang's example and combat the old education approach. The key message was that the old education system, especially the Confucius philosophy and practice, needed to be revolutionized, and the teachers needed to be reformed and re-educated. Respect for teachers and emphasis on formal education changed for the worse throughout the entire country.

At Lianlian's elementary school, the administrators and teachers never disciplined Gao Qiang. As the Huang Shuai movement continued, they became careful and timid when dealing with students.

Then came the big character papers being posted on the walls of the buildings. Most of them were anonymous and appeared overnight. Accusations were made about teachers, administrators, or school events. Some of them described instances that had occurred a long time before. No one ever dared take them down. Eventually, either the wind or rain would wash them away, or fresh paper would cover them up once there were no empty spots left.

The atmosphere on campus was tense, and no one could concentrate on teaching or learning.

Fortunately, no one tied up or beat any of the teachers in public. But Lianlian heard on the radio that such violence had happened elsewhere, with some teachers humiliated so gravely that they committed suicide.

As usual, Lianlian reported every detail of the event to Jun.

"Teachers and older adults always deserve our respect, no matter what. Not all traditional values are bad," Jun reminded Lianlian along the way.

The Huang Shuai movement had a profound effect on China's education system, its moral values, and its respect for educators. It affected an entire generation and maybe even more. A thousand-year-old tradition was destroyed in the blink of an eye, and it would take generations to restore and recover what had been lost.

20

JUN DATING

Among middle-aged people, there were more single men, and fewer single women. At the tender age of 38, Jun looked vibrant, pretty, and much younger than her age. Her confidence and intelligence made her stand out in any crowd. Single men showed a strong interest in her. Some approached her directly. Some tried to make a connection through a third or a fourth person. People regarded her as a highly valuable candidate for a second marriage, and Jun was open to the idea of remarrying.

Uncle Wei had a good reason to spend time around Jun. He dubbed himself the chief of construction for Jun's side house. After that was done, he continued to visit whenever he was in town, which was often, and helped with many chores. He broke apart large pieces of coal and helped stack winter supplies when the institute distributed them. The girls were happiest when he volunteered to visit the underground cellar. He even admonished a neighbor boy when he called the girls insulting names.

But Jun never thought of him as a possibility. Once she recognized his obvious intentions, she told him to leave and never come back, to avoid any gossip. He held back tears when he said goodbye to

Lianlian and Shanshan, who had treated him as an uncle, a family member.

Lianlian often imagined what life might have been like if he had lived with them. No one would ever say bad things to them because Uncle Wei could scare them. Her mom wouldn't have to do any hard labor because he wouldn't allow it. And he would continue reading books together with the girls, something her own mother never did.

A college professor visited for several months. He was slim but tall and good-looking. When Lianlian first met him, he looked familiar to her. After that, she remembered the pictures of Ge Yan-Shao in old photographs. From the stories Jun had told over the years, Lianlian sensed she had regrets, and figured that was why she constantly revisited the old photos.

The professor's four children were grown, meeting one of Jun's criteria: no young children at home. His wife had died of an illness. He stated he wanted to find someone educated. His visits became lengthy, sometimes stretching into the night. A few times, sounds from the kitchen awoke Lianlian in the middle of the night, and she realized he was still in the house.

One day, Jun told Lianlian he wanted to talk to her after school. Lianlian set to work on her geometry homework. The professor sat opposite Lianlian on the other side of the desk.

He pulled his chair forward. "Your mom suggested I talk to you alone, as you have opinions and ideas, whereas your sister is easy to please."

Easy to please? Right, Shanshan had shown me a small pencil sharpener he'd given her. Had he been trying to buy her off?

Giving him a polite nod, Lianlian continued to draw a cylinder.

"I used to be good at geometry, too, when I was in junior school."

"Do you need to know geometry to be an English professor?" Lianlian asked. At one point, Jun had suggested he teach her English. That hadn't happened yet.

"No. Geometry is just part of a general education. Everyone needs to learn it in school."

"Do you still remember it? Can you answer a question I have?"

"Unfortunately, I've forgotten most of it. I can't help you."

He didn't even ask what my question was. Mom would have asked that first before deciding whether she could help me.

Lianlian continued working on her homework.

He paused a moment and said,

"Your mom and I plan to get married. Are you fine with that?"

Lianlian had sensed they'd been getting close.

"I just want my mom to be happy. If she is, I have no objection."

She picked up the eraser and cleaned up a line to redraw it.

"Very well. Continue with your homework. It's important to do well in school."

I know that, and I don't need anyone to give me such empty reminders. Lianlian mentally rolled her eyes. Somehow, she didn't believe he was the right fit for her mom. He didn't give Lianlian the feeling that he cared for Jun that much. Lianlian often found him superficial; he seemed to care only about appearance, not the meaning of things. But if her mom liked him, fine.

The professor stopped coming soon after that. Lianlian became uneasy. *Did I mess up their relationship?*

"I have a meeting this evening. You two take care of your dinner." That normally meant Jun was on a date.

"Are you meeting the professor?" Lianlian asked nervously, but he'd be here in the house if he were the one Jun was seeing. Jun didn't bring home every new man she met.

"No. We ended things. He has a handicap. I helped put on his shirt the other day and saw that his right shoulder was uneven. He said it was a sports injury from college. I cannot marry someone who has a handicap. Shanshan, don't forget to do your homework after dinner."

That might explain why he didn't help Jun carry the bike one day when rainwater blocked the entry to the yard gate. Uncle Wei would have helped in a heartbeat. Lianlian wasn't sorry they ended their relationship, but she wasn't sure it was justified. His body looked fine.

Later, Jun confided to Lianlian that the professor cared little about Jun and the girls. He looked forward to the girls leaving the house. He also expected Jun to take care of most household chores because she'd only attended a vocational school, while he had a college degree.

What a way to insult my mom!

Mr. Chen often visited their new home. Mr. Chen was married, but his family lived in Tianjin, a neighboring city to Beijing. He continued working at the same institute where Jun used to work and was the only former colleague of hers who would bring news and gossip.

Mr. Chen came to their home after dinner every day. He sat there and sometimes said something, but most of the time kept silent. Lianlian sat on one side of the only desk to do her homework. He sat on the other side. When Shanshan needed it to do her homework, he moved to a stool by the stove. Jun sat on the kang sewing or knitting, answering him here and there, but mostly ignoring him. Around bedtime, Jun would say, "Time to go now," and off he'd go.

The girls created a nickname for him: Heavy Butt Chen. They didn't hate him but hardly liked him either. He didn't help with anything at home or with the girls' homework. He just sat there.

One day, Mr. Chen came again. Out of the blue, Jun suggested, "Maybe you can teach Lianlian Chinese calligraphy. She might be very good at it."

Mr. Chen asked for Lianlian's Chinese homework booklet and examined it. In his slow and monotonous tone, he said, "I can see that. She has good wrist control, critical for writing calligraphy."

Lianlian was not eager to do calligraphy. The Chinese classes in elementary school had once covered calligraphy. Preparing the ink was a lot of work. One had to add water to a special saucer and smash a piece of inkstone on the saucer to produce the ink. Afterward, one must wash the brush and the saucer and let them dry for the next time. Although the materials and the brush cost little, they were not free. Plus, they needed special paper.

"It will give her an edge, having a special and valuable talent, when she grows up," Jun said.

"True. With so many people, one must have a specialty to stand out and be desirable to employers or organizations." Mr. Chen followed.

Hmm, that sounds reasonable. Lianlian agreed to try it.

She visited Mr. Chen's place on a Sunday. It was small but neat. He put the paper, ink, and brush on the desk. He explained a few things and showed her how to do it on paper by holding her hand.

That made Lianlian uncomfortable. But she wasn't sure if she was being oversensitive. She didn't report it to her mother—when Jun asked, she said everything was fine.

When the next scheduled time came, Lianlian came up with several excuses—like doing homework and feeding the chickens.

"Is something wrong?" asked Jun.

"I don't like him holding my hand to show me how to write. Plus, his calligraphy isn't that good."

That was the end of Heavy Butt Chen's visits.

Jun met several other men after that. Most were much older than she was. Among them, several were nice and treated her well, but her standards were high. Any potential partner had to be a graduate of a top university. He must be handsome and tall, have no young children at home, and earn a high income or hold a high-status position at work.

Lianlian's overall observation was that her mother put more weight on "hardware" conditions than on a man's heart. The degree, status, and good looks could bring pride but didn't guarantee the man would be loving. It also seemed she was looking for a twin of Lianlian's father, or an old image of Ge Yan-Shao.

She thought to herself. *I would not look for a handsome guy who's nasty. I wonder if a less handsome guy might be kinder.*

21

Junior High School

Lianlian entered junior high school at 12 in 1975.

The city assigned students to junior high schools based on where they lived. Lianlian's school's name was Hohhot No. 2 High School. It was a step up in several ways from the elementary school. Her cohort comprised 21 classes, each with 50 students. The campus housed four grades: two grades for high school and the second and third grades for junior high. The elementary school's sixth grade was equivalent to the first grade in junior high. During recess, a sea of people filled the playground, even though the junior and high school divisions had different recess times.

The campus was huge and divided into three different sections. The first one was within a courtyard of surrounding walls, where four rows of flat, one-story buildings hosted four classrooms each. This was the original campus of the school, established in 1947. The second section had three rows of flat buildings, each with five classrooms. These buildings employed stoves with pipes to heat the rooms during the winter. Lianlian's classroom was in one of those buildings.

The third and newest section was an L-shaped, four-story build-ing that had water-based heaters in each room. Administrators and teachers occupied the first floor of one wing. The higher grades were on the upper floors. By the third year of junior high school, Lianlian's class had moved from the flat building to the first floor of the tall building.

Lianlian's junior high homeroom teacher was Teacher Tuan, who taught math. In his late 30s, he welcomed a baby son with his wife and raised a young girl, whom his wife had brought to the mar-riage, as his own. Sometimes, Teacher Tuan carried the boy on his shoulders when he came to the classroom in the evenings or on informal occasions. Teacher Tuan was of medium build, wore a pair of thick glasses, and spoke with a distinctive Shanxi accent. He was disciplined, held traditional values, and was serious all the time, especially in front of the students and their families. He didn't hold back his opinions if he felt something was wrong or inappropriate, regardless of whether the perceived wrongdoers were the authorities, his colleagues, parents, or students. Everyone was afraid of him—in-cluding Lianlian.

At the first parent-teacher conference, Teacher Tuan announced a new morning routine. Every student needed to arrive an hour early to run with him before self-study.

There was murmuring among the parents. One raised his hand. "Kids need to have enough sleep."

"Put them in bed earlier at night," Teacher Tuan replied.

"My son has never run, not even during physical education class-es," said another parent.

Teacher Tuan was firm. "Then it's time for him to run."

Jun looked at Lianlian with worry. After the conference, she approached Teacher Tuan.

"My daughter has a condition where her heart beats unevenly. I'm not sure if she can run."

"Did the doctor say she shouldn't run?" asked Teacher Tuan.

"No, he just said to keep monitoring her to see if her condition worsens."

"Then she should run. It may help."

In the fall, students could get up early and get to school during daylight hours. The class formed four columns and many rows. If a student was late, he or she just joined the end of the row. The playground's running track was 400 meters per lap. With Teacher Tuan in the lead, the students would run four laps, keeping up with his fast pace.

On the first day, Lianlian got to school early enough that she had to wait for Teacher Tuan. When he arrived, he had on a light top, a pair of shorts, and sneakers. Most of the students didn't have any proper running gear. Lianlian had her regular clothes and a pair of sneakers that were hand-me-downs from a friend of Jun's. After running, Lianlian had to wear the same clothes for the rest of the school day.

The class formed the lines by height, as they normally did during recess. Lianlian was in front since she was short. Soon after they started, her heart jumped so fast that she was afraid it might burst out of her chest. She slowed, which put her at the end of the team, and then fell behind everyone. She kept running a few more meters and rested by the side of the track to catch her breath. Every twenty meters was a struggling student resting. Teacher Tuan and the team never slowed or stopped. When they passed Lianlian on the next lap, she joined the end of the line. But soon, she had to drop out again. She tried to run by herself at a slower pace. But she had to stop again to suppress the uneasy sensation of her heart screaming.

The first class of the day was a self-study class. Lianlian sat in her seat, sweaty, like other students. As usual, Teacher Tuan came to the classroom. He had changed his clothes and was wearing normal teacher garb. Lianlian was afraid he might criticize those who hadn't been able to keep up with the running. But he didn't. It was just a regular self-study class. He paced from aisle to aisle and checked what each student was doing. Most of them either did their homework or previewed the materials for the day.

Lianlian made a mental note that she should do better.

The next day, she had a hard time getting up because her legs, back, and feet were hurting. But she arrived at school in time for the run. The class was smaller. The running was the same. Lianlian dropped out twice but rejoined the group to finish.

On the last day of the week, Teacher Tuan praised the runners and warned those who didn't come. It was obvious he'd meant what he said about everyone running in the morning.

Lianlian was relieved that by then her body didn't bother her as much. Despite experiencing many moments when she thought her body or heart was in trouble, seeing her classmates continue to run made her keep going. Staying with the group became a motivator. If she were to run by herself, she might have stopped more often or quit entirely.

One month passed. There was only one student who consistently missed the morning run—Gao Qiang, the bully from Lianlian's elementary school.

One sunny morning, Teacher Tuan announced, "We will run off-campus today."

The entire class followed him to the street. Their neat formation of running in unison attracted attention from those riding bikes or walking on the sidewalk. Lianlian felt a sense of pride to be part of the team.

After a few turns, they arrived at a house with a big yard.

Teacher Tuan pounded on the gate. A few minutes later, a tall and bulky young man opened the gate.

"We are here to wake up Gao Qiang to join the class morning run." Teacher Tuan said.

"Wait here," the young man looked puzzled and annoyed.

A few minutes later, Gao Qiang came out. His eyes were struggling to adjust to the light.

"The entire class is waiting here until you join us so that we can go back to school," said Teacher Tuan.

Lianlian was worried that Gao Qiang might snap and do something dangerous. Plus, the young man who'd opened the gate was his older brother, and he looked very dangerous too.

But Gao Qiang did not snap. His face turned red. He shook his head, went inside, and came out many minutes later with his schoolbag across his upper body. The entire class ran back to school.

Gao Qiang never missed another run during the second month. Perhaps the entire class standing behind Teacher Tuan made him ashamed, or perhaps he had become more mature. But just when

Lianlian thought even a student like him could change for the better, he stopped coming to school. There were rumors that his father had taken early retirement to save the spot for Gao Qiang at his factory.

By the end of the second month, every student could keep up with the group during the entire run. The morning run lasted throughout junior high school.

When they tested her again, doctors could no longer detect the uneven rhythms in Lianlian's heart.

Students had limited opportunities for socializing. There were no public places for them to go, and no homes big enough to hold many people. Starting in junior high, students would visit each other during the Spring Festival break. One would visit another student's home. They'd bike to a third student's home. Together, they'd continue to a fourth student. There was no prior communication and no announcement. They just did it. Moms often warmly invited them inside and offered delicious treats. They never got hungry during the entire day's trip. Everyone knew where everyone else lived. They saw other groups of students biking on the street, too. It was a normal thing students did, from junior high to high school. During that time, girls gathered with girls, and boys with boys. This continued after the students went to college and came back home to visit. By that time, it was co-ed, and boys and girls visited each other as a group.

Lianlian did not have a bike. In the first year of junior high, a classmate carried her on the backseat.

"Can I come, too?" Shanshan wanted to join the group.

"This is my class, and you don't know anyone," said Lianlian.

For the first time, she wanted to be just her, not carrying her little sister. These were HER classmates.

But another classmate insisted she wanted to take Shanshan.

The following year, Shanshan wanted to come again.

Lianlian felt a strong urge to break free from her little sister for such events.

"Wait for your own classmates, and ride with them," Lianlian snapped.

"They won't come," said Shanshan.

"How do you know?" Lianlian followed.

"They won't. I want to go with your classmates," insisted Shanshan.

"She's welcome. I'll carry her!" One classmate nodded to Shanshan, who jumped into the backseat before Lianlian could object.

In the evening, Lianlian and Shanshan returned home.

"Did any of Shanshan's classmates come by?" Lianlian asked Jun.

"Nope," Jun answered.

During junior high, Shanshan never had her classmates visit, not even once. She was a loner, just like when she was at the daycare center. But she was Lianlian's shadow. It was not surprising that Lianlian's classmates wanted to carry Shanshan. They adored her and called her "Lianlian #2" when they saw her on campus.

Lianlian accepted the fact that she could not get rid of her little sister at such social events or in other situations. Her annoyance disappeared.

22

LEI FENG, WORKERS, AND PEASANTS

School was never boring. There was always something going on. Besides academics, students were doing a lot of things that were tied to political campaigns. Chairman Mao's slogan, "Learn from Dazhai in Agriculture; Learn from Daqing in Industry; Everyone Should Learn from the People's Liberation Army," affected every corner of China.

In school, students had special activities as requirements to learn from workers, peasants, and soldiers.

The school arranged many activities to help students learn from Lei Feng. "Follow the example of Lei Feng" was a national campaign that originated in 1963 and lasted many decades. Everyone had heard of Lei Feng, a private in the People's Liberation Army. He became a role model for his altruism and for living his life under Chairman Mao's ideals. Students learned many of his stories of selflessly helping others in work and daily life. For example, he'd help elder people to cross the streets, carry bags for others, and assist co-workers with their jobs. He had read Chairman Mao's work and had journaled on his understanding and applications of Maoism. He passed away at a young age, but his name and image continued to shine over many generations.

One day, Teacher Tuan announced, "We'll continue the campion of learning from Lei Feng. Bring brooms and dust pans from home tomorrow. Our class is assigned to sweep the grounds in a nearby bus station."

Although mostly positive when people mentioned Lei Feng's name, others would sometimes sarcastically remark, "What a living Lei Feng you are."

Such comments shocked Lianlian when she did good deeds, like turning in the money she'd found on campus, or extending help to others with little expectation of reward. To her, these were just the right things to do and had little to do with following Lei Feng. The remarks also made her sad because it seemed people did not believe in doing good things and only did them for show.

One way of learning from peasants was going to the countryside to help farmers prepare for planting or harvesting. Such events took a whole day or days as field trips away from the classroom. To Lianlian, these events were fun. Students got to spend a whole day outside, and they might bring some fresh produce home—something that would make Lianlian very proud.

During one such trip, the students went to help harvest radishes in May. At lunchtime, everyone was excited to sit in circles, showcase their lunches, and brag about special foods their moms had prepared for them.

Lianlian sat with her best friend, Li Ling, away from most of the other students. Teacher Tuan came over to check on them and saw

Lianlian had a corn bun, a tea egg, and preserved vegetables. This was just her usual lunch food. Li Ling's food wasn't super special either. That might be one reason the two of them were friends. Neither of them cared about material possessions or superficial matters. Neither of them liked to gossip about others like most girls did. And both of them put effort into doing well in school.

Teacher Tuan walked away with a strange expression. He returned a few minutes later while Lianlian was still pondering the look on his face. He gave Lianlian and Li Ling each a delicious dessert his wife had packed.

On every future field trip, the two girls would get some nice food from him. That didn't go well with the rest of the classmates. Lianlian and Li Ling both earned the nickname "teacher's pets."

Students visited factories. The school connected with local workshops, and students showed up, usually in groups. Such events could last one afternoon, several afternoons, or even several whole days in a row.

In 1976, when Lianlian was 13, she and her classmates had to spend one week working in a place that produced concrete bricks. They needed to have evaluation forms filled out by site supervisors to pass. Her group had six people. Their job was to load bricks onto vehicles. They had to ride their bikes to the factory. That was a challenge for her because she didn't have a bike. One of her group members, Lihua, who lived not too far from her, would come to pick her up in the morning, then drop her off after work. Lianlian sat in the back seat.

"Don't thank me—I'm just learning from Lei Feng!" Lihua said with a laugh.

On the fifth day of their assignment, Lihua said she couldn't give Lianlian a ride home that day because she had another arrangement.

"Don't worry, Lihua. I'll ask others to help me." It would have taken Lianlian more than an hour to walk home.

Hong, a tall girl in her group, heard her. "Allow me to offer you a lift. But if you don't mind, we'll do something first before I drop you at home," she winked.

The "something" was to follow Lihua and a male classmate named Weitong. Besides Hong and Lianlian, another girl from their group joined them.

"What's going on?" Lianlian asked. The two of them knew more than she did.

"They've been staring at each other since day one. They seem to like each other. Maybe they're dating." Hong pedaled hard with excitement in her voice. The three of them were about 100 meters behind Lihua and Weidong, who rode side by side with almost two meters between them. They tried to make it seem like they didn't know each other.

Wow, this was big news. Boys and girls were not supposed to talk to each other, let alone do things together. It was considered dirty, evil, and just bad.

Lianlian admired the keen, perceptive eyes of Hong and the other girl. Maybe she hadn't noticed such things because she'd been too busy being the group leader and getting things done.

They followed Lihua and Weitong down several major streets. Then they lost the two after one sharp turn. After circling a few times, they gave up.

The next day, Lianlian paid close attention to Lihua and Weitong. There was indeed something going on between them. They'd blush whenever they glanced at each other, which was often.

After finishing work, the three of them followed Lihua and Weitong again. The pair were riding side by side again, but much closer this time. The three girls tailed them for as long as they could. At one intersection, Lihua turned one way and Weidong another.

Hong dropped Lianlian off at her house and then looked into her eyes. "Are you going to report it to Teacher Tuan?"

"Should I? They did nothing except leave work together. I don't think they even talked to each other."

"Well, it's up to you," Hong shrugged after thinking for a moment.

The following Monday, everyone was back in the classroom. Lianlian heard constant gossip about Lihua and Weitong. Poor Lihua lowered her head whenever there were people around. Lianlian felt bad about her being shamed by others, which reminded her of how she and her sister had been shamed by others. But Lianlian thought there was a difference: Lihua had earned the shame with her own behavior.

Watch what you do, or others will shame you, she reminded herself.

Lianlian heard no fresh stories about Lihua and Weitong after that. Either nothing happened, or people didn't pass such news to her. But she learned one had to be careful when dealing with boys, so as not to get a terrible reputation.

But why did the two of them want to ride together? Lianlian wondered. *Why did they blush when looking at each other?* Her awareness of romantic love wouldn't come until much later.

Another day, another announcement from Teacher Tuan.

"Sign up for one of the two events for the next two days: one group to go to the hospital and one to go to the museum. Both places are doing maintenance and need extra help."

The museum?! That intrigued Lianlian. She passed the museum every day on her way to school, although she hadn't been inside for a while. The museum always held a feeling of authority for her. Now she had a chance to visit it again, and not just as a regular visitor, but to help it!

As soon as Teacher Tuan's announcement ended, she signed up for the museum. She was among ten students — five girls and five boys.

A worker directed everyone, "Boys, you are to go up to the top to clean the debris around the horse. Girls, you stay down here to clean the floor."

Around the horse?! Is that even possible? It is so high and tall when looking from the street level!

Lianlian was excited. She had considered the white horse to be spectacular, majestic, and masculine. She wanted to get as close to the horse as possible.

Lianlian carefully approached the worker. "Shushu, could I go to the top, too?"

The worker examined her skinny body. "No, you cannot. You'll be scared to ride up that high and walk around the top floor to do anything. It will be just trouble for everyone involved."

A boy approached the worker, too.

"My mom said I should not go to high places. Can I stay down here to work on the lower floors?"

The worker looked at him and nodded. "Sure, if you want, you can stay down here."

Lianlian stepped forward. "I can take his place to go up. I promise I won't be a trouble."

"No. Too much danger for a girl."

"Please. I just want to see the horse up close. I don't know if I will ever have another chance to see it this close."

"Tell you what. Once everyone completes their tasks and does a great job, I will take anyone interested to the top for a tour."

The next afternoon, when the students were to be dismissed, Lianlian approached the worker. "Shushu, is it time for us to have a tour to see the horse now?"

"Okay, I'll make good on my promise. Who's up for it? Follow me."

Three girls passed on the opportunity, and only one other girl and Lianlian went to the service elevator.

This was the first time Lianlian had taken an elevator to such a tall place! The elevator arrived at a large room piled high with building materials.

The worker took the two girls to a wooden ladder. It was a basic ladder and had no solid support, just some steps hanging from two long wood beams that reached from an opening at the top.

"You can stop here if you're afraid of climbing the ladder." He smiled at Lianlian and the other girl.

"I'll wait for you two here. I'm afraid to look down through the steps," the other girl said.

"That's the key—don't look down when climbing. Just up," the worker said.

"But what about climbing down? I'm going to stay here and wait," the girl said.

Lianlian hesitated.

The ladder is indeed scary. What if I don't hold my feet steady and I slip? But what about the chance to see the horse this close? And what is the worst that can happen? I fall to the floor on this level and break a leg? Nah, it won't happen if I'm careful.

She straightened her back and said, "I'll go with you."

The worker nodded in appreciation. "You climb in front of me. If you fall, I can catch you. But keep in mind, it's not that bad. The repair workers have to carry heavy stuff and climb the ladders up and down. Your four classmates did it by going up there to gather debris and pass it down."

Lianlian took a deep breath and stepped onto the ladder.

It wasn't bad at all! She reached the opening and climbed up to the outside.

The strong wind almost knocked her down. The worker caught her in time and put her steadily on her feet.

In front of her, about ten meters away, was a platform where the horse stood. It was a gigantic creature, almost as tall as several stories. It was so big that Lianlian had to raise her head all the way to see all its parts.

One of its front legs revealed dark metal colors. Someone had wrapped its tail in a dark material.

Lianlian was shocked to see how rough the entire being was. The surface was lumpy; the muscles stood out like rough edges of mountains, and the color was not pure white but dirty. It looked nothing like what she'd seen at street level.

She stared at the horse for a long time.

"Is this the original horse?" She asked the worker.

"No. This was the second one."

"What happened to the first one?"

"Well, the museum was built in 1957 with an empty top. Then a horse was added to make it more interesting and artistic. But it was facing north where the Blue Mountains are. Someone noted the horse appeared to be running toward the Soviet Union, which bordered us and controlled Mongolia. So, that horse was replaced by this one, running toward Beijing."

Lianlian was fascinated by the story.

"Have you seen the first one? Was it the same as this one?"

"I might have but I can't remember what it was like. Who'd pay attention to such details?"

"This one is dirty."

"This is just maintenance, patching up here and painting there. Up here under the sun, the elements can damage the statue."

"Its surface is not as smooth as I thought."

"That's because you were looking at it from a distance. See how big its horseshoe is, bigger than my head," the worker gestured.

Compared to the horse, Lianlian's tiny body was almost non-existent, and the worker's body was barely noticeable.

Lianlian was troubled. Not quite disappointed, but this piece challenged her image of the majestic white horse.

Something can be so different when looked at up close. Or something can be so deceiving when looked at from a distance.

The worker broke her train of thought. "Ready to go down now?"

"Sure."

"I'm going down the ladder first. Once I get down, you come."

Lianlian looked at the bottom of the ladder and could not put her foot on the steps. The ladder suddenly became twice as long as she remembered. Up here, things seemed to be out of proportion.

"It's okay. Don't be afraid. Turn around, look at the ladder or look up, then put your feet down one rung at a time, as if you were climbing up. Just don't look down."

Lianlian followed his instructions. One step at a time, she reached the floor.

She was quiet on the elevator. The thrill of riding the elevator had disappeared.

"Do you wish you hadn't come up to see the horse?" asked the worker.

Lianlian thought for a moment.

"I'm glad I came up. I learned something about the horse that I didn't know before. Plus, I got to ride the elevator and learned how to climb down a long ladder."

23

ACUPUNCTURE AND OVERALL PLANNING

Acupuncture was widely practiced by "barefoot doctors," health care providers who underwent basic medical training and worked in the countryside. Many of them were Down-to-the-Countryside youngsters who had an education. The barefoot name referred to the fact that they became peasants and farmers who often worked barefoot.

People other than medical professionals often practiced acupuncture. Many times, Jun would press acupoints or use needles for minor issues such as headaches, nausea, or stomach pains for herself and the two girls.

Teacher Tuan offered informal classes in acupuncture during afternoon recess. Lianlian was eager to join. Half of the students in the class attended regularly for weeks. They received silver needles in various sizes and alcohol balls from the nurse's office. One student's mom had access to medical supplies and provided them for free.

Students learned common acupoints and their functions. Lianlian particularly liked two of them, one on the hand and one on the wrist, because they would ease pain and nausea, two common conditions—especially for her. It was thrilling to break her skin and then push the needles deep inside these acupoints. There was no pain, but a powerful sensation of numbness, soreness, or tightening.

Students also practiced on each other. The trust they placed in each other and in Teacher Tuan was amazing. Later, Lianlian learned things could easily go wrong with acupuncture and lead to devastating consequences, including being paralyzed.

"Attention, students." An intercom message rang during the first self-study class. "This afternoon, we will have a visit from two scientists, who will introduce two scientific methods to you. Line up and bring your chairs to the playground."

That was the first and only time the school hosted such a large lecture at the school. The only place that could hold that many students was the playground. There were two sessions, one for junior and one for high school students.

Excitement was in the air. Students lined up as they did for their regular recess, with each student two arms-lengths apart for stretching and kicking. On a simple brick platform about one meter high, two gentlemen sat behind a table. An administrator introduced them. Theirs were not household names, but they had made significant contributions, according to the introductions.

The lecture lasted 45 minutes. There were no visuals. One had to pay attention to what the scientists were saying. Fortunately, they were both good at repeating and giving unique examples.

Lianlian remained intrigued the entire time. It amazed her that the scientific methods they were describing had many applications and yielded significant results. For Lianlian, there were three main takeaways from the lecture.

The "overall planning method" refers to planning as a whole. For any project or undertaking, one should identify all the parts and understand their relationships. In particular, one should know which parts were bottlenecks and which parts could be done in parallel. If a part needed extra time, one should get it started sooner so that the entire project could be finished on time. By identifying the best sequence for the tasks, starting the longest task first, and doing other tasks concurrently, efficiency could be improved.

The "optimization method" was about finding out how to improve by using the least experimentation. More was not better. There was an optimal number of experiments that could lead to the best results. For example, making steel requires adding coal, but how much should be added to get the best results? The optimization method offered a guide to efficiently figuring out that number.

The golden ratio was an intriguing concept. It described dividing a whole into two parts. The ratio of the smaller part to the larger was the same as the ratio of the larger part to the whole, resulting in a 0.618 ratio. Although in applications one might not do an exact 0.618 division, understanding the meaning of this ratio was beneficial. For example, standing in the middle of the stage was less attractive than standing around the Golden Ratio, the spot roughly 0.618% or one-third from one side. Even books had a ratio between their length and width of about 0.618. There were many examples in famous works of art and architecture where ratios were 0.618.

In retrospect, such topics belonged in college mathematics courses. China's famous mathematician, Hua Luogeng, had led a campaign to apply mathematical theories and concepts to manage real-world problems in production, farming, service, and daily life. To be effective in the campaign, Hua Luogeng selected the dual methods—overall planning and optimization—and introduced them everywhere in plain and easy-to-understand language and examples. This campaign, endorsed by Chairman Mao in 1964, continued for many years and had a tremendous impact on the nation's development in all sectors and industries.

The students were beneficiaries of that campaign.

The two scientists did a great job of introducing system-related concepts and applications. They resonated with Lianlian and fascinated her. After that, she applied what they taught her in her daily life whenever situations call for it. For example, when cooking a meal of rice and a vegetable dish, the order makes a difference. If she washed the vegetables, then cooked them, and then cooked the rice, it could take a long time for the meal to be ready. If she cooked the rice (30–40 minutes) and then prepared the vegetables while it cooked, she could finish the meal much faster.

Lianlian found that applying these methods made doing any task more fun. She would start with an analysis first before undertaking any small steps. The analysis stage was something she looked forward to. Her nickname of "Ms. Efficiency" from her friends and family members might have something to do with the way she applied the overall planning method as much as possible in her life.

The 0.618 rule would guide her on many aesthetic-related projects and endeavors, too. The clearest and most frequent application was in photography. Instead of being in the middle, the focal point should lie roughly one-third from the edge of the frame.

Lianlian discovered she was fascinated by topics that were logical and had real-world implications.

24

PASSING OF ZHOU, ZHU, AND MAO

1976 was a disturbing year for China. The mother of one of Jun's friends, who had a reputation for knowing everything that happened in the universe, had seen three enormous stars falling out of the sky.

On a cold and dry winter day in January 1976, the radio played sad music, followed by the announcement that China's Premier Zhou Enlai had passed away at age 77. That was the first time Lianlian had heard such music—funeral music—on the radio. For many days, there was no other music on the radio but funeral music.

Jun pulled out some leftover black cloth and made three armbands. When Lianlian got to school, she found everyone was wearing a black armband over their right sleeve.

The school designated the largest cafeteria/performing hall as the remembrance hall. A huge black-and-white portrait hung in the middle of the wall on the stage. Layer after layer of funeral wreaths surrounded the podium. Classes took turns visiting the remembrance hall. Students and teachers stood for the duration of the funeral music, with their heads lowered to show respect.

Every organization did similar things. Either individually or in organized groups, people visited places where Zhou Enlai's portraits were surrounded by funeral wreaths. Jun took Lianlian and Shanshan to visit the museum, which was free to the public for this special occasion. Photos, articles, and artworks about Zhou Enlai filled the entire place.

Lianlian saw her mother weep many times. She noticed many grown-ups shed tears. Lianlian cried, too. Growing up, she had heard his name and seen his image so many times, especially in images where he met with leaders and diplomats from other countries. Tall and handsome, he was always in a Chinese suit, with a pleasant and respectable manner, never arrogant and never self-effacing.

Lianlian trusted him unquestioningly. That might be why her view of the United States of America changed from negative to positive. Since early childhood, Lianlian learned that there were two major enemies of China: The Soviet Union and the United States of America.

Jun told her that the Soviet Union had been a big brother to China during Jun's school years. The foreign language taught at the school was Russian, and Jun learned it at her vocational school. She'd had little chance to practice because the relationship between the Soviet Union and China quickly worsened after she began working as an engineer. The Soviet Union became one of China's biggest enemies. "Soviet Revisionism" was the term Lianlian had learned to refer to the Soviet Union.

The other biggest enemy was America. Lianlian remembered following the slogans of "Bring Down American Imperialism" and

"Knock Down the Paper Tiger," even though she didn't quite understand the meanings behind those slogans.

But Lianlian's impression of America changed when Zhou Enlai welcomed Henry Kissinger in Beijing. Soon after that, Zhou Enlai greeted President Nixon. That event brought the notion of "Ping-Pong Diplomacy," which replaced the reference to the "Paper Tiger."

If Premier Zhou meets and greets Americans, then America may not be bad, Lianlian concluded. It might have been no coincidence that in middle and high schools, students' foreign language studies changed to English.

As Jun and the girls continued their tour of the museum, Jun reminded the girls, "Not once was Premier Zhou ever associated with anything bad or questionable. Not once."

Lianlian was glad to learn that. She had engraved Zhou's image in her mind as a kind, reliable, and perfect parent of the enormous family that was the entire nation. But knowing he was not with the people anymore was heartbreaking.

April 5th was the nation's Memorial Day in China. People would pay their respects to their dead loved ones by visiting their graves, burning paper money, or setting up a little memorial shrine with photos.

But Lianlian had never seen such a large-scale celebration of life as when the nation honored Zhou Enlai's life.

Lianlian heard murmurs among grown-ups, including her mom. But every time they noticed her presence, they would stop talking.

At school, students in higher grades brought handwritten poems to share. People copied them and shared them widely. Lianlian didn't quite understand most of the poems' significance besides the recognition that they were artistically beautiful. But she sensed there was an invisible war going on. Those who passed around the poems were defending or fighting for Zhou Enlai. She didn't know who the enemy was, but that didn't bother her. She'd defend and fight for Zhou Enlai, too. His enemy—whatever it was—would be hers, too!

One of those poems was soul-shaking. Lianlian remembered it for a long time. Although it's hard to translate into English without losing its beauty and meaning, here is an approximation:

> *Saddened, I hear wolves screaming.*
> *My weeping was accompanied by jackals' laughing.*
> *Shedding tears to honor my hero,*
> *Ready with my unsheathed sword shining.*

Lianlian showed this poem to her mother. Jun had seen it already.

"What does it mean? Who are the wolves and jackals?"

"You are too young. No need to know. Just be careful not to stand out among the crowd," Jun answered.

"Too bad there's no place to visit him."

"He was a humble person who wanted no one to worship him. He just wanted to serve the people. It's a great thing that he didn't leave his body to be mistreated. Cremation worked out brilliantly. With his ashes spread over the rivers and mountains, they live with everyone," Jun said proudly. She continued, "He was a real man, a true human being. I wish more people were like him."

Lianlian recalled her mother's scorn when someone mentioned the remarriages of most Communist Party founders after the wars. Jun had said, "But Zhou Enlai didn't."

Lianlian also realized something. *If people want to remember you, there is no need for a grave, a tombstone, or a physical object. They'll remember you in their hearts. When I die, I want to be cremated and have my ashes spread, too. That will save land and save loved ones' trouble tending to a grave.*

The second star that fell from the sky was Zhu De, one of the founding generals and the Head of State of China. He passed away in July at 89. Although the funereal music was on the radio, the nation was numb. Schools were already on summer break, so there were no organized events for mourning.

September 9, 1976 became one of the most important days in China's history: Mao Zedong, the CCP chairman and the founding president of China, died at 82.

School had just resumed for the new academic year. Students didn't have regular classes for days. Instead, they took part in various activities to remember and celebrate Mao. Besides paying their respects in the remembrance hall multiple times each day and in the playground during recess, they also wrote poems and essays to express their feelings and thoughts. Some of them read their compositions out loud in class, which always brought tears to everyone present. Some compositions made it to the bulletin board at the back of the classroom. The campus bulletin boards displayed the most well-regarded pieces.

Mao's passing deeply saddened Lianlian. It felt like a part of her had died, too. Ever since she could remember, she had heard the words "Chairman Mao" every day in various situations. She saw his photos and portraits everywhere. People wore pins of his portrait on their clothes, and Lianlian felt lucky she had some pins, too. Everyone, including students, studied his philosophies at work or school. Lianlian had several red books of his excerpted sayings, just like everyone else. His poems were magnificent, with literary value, and students studied and memorized them in Chinese literary classes. His calligraphy was pure art, and people hung prints of his calligraphic works as decorations at home. Over the past ten years, Chairman Mao had been a significant and inseparable part of Lianlian's life. Subconsciously, she'd never imagined he was mortal, just like everyone else. To learn that he had died was like finding out her world was not what she thought it was.

It felt comforting to mourn with family, teachers, and classmates. Growing up together, Lianlian's peers had very similar experiences to her regarding having Mao in their lives. It felt good to know that she wasn't alone in her feelings.

Shanshan was sad too, but not as strongly as Lianlian. She went with the flow and did what was required or expected of her.

Jun was mostly silent, even when Lianlian or Shanshan were saddened. That was a huge contrast to her reaction to Zhou Enlai's passing. Lianlian wanted to know why. But every time she brought up matters regarding Chairman Mao, Jun would divert the topic somewhere else. A few attempts later, Lianlian concluded Jun was not as close emotionally to Chairman Mao as she was to Zhou Enlai.

Lianlian passed the museum every day. She saw people going in and coming out in groups. Jun's decision not to take them to the Chairman Mao exhibit at the museum made her think her mom knew secrets she didn't, and those secrets might be bad.

A month after Mao died, the Communist Party announced the capture of the Gang of Four via radio and newspapers. Jiang Qing, Mao's wife, was the leader and considered an enemy of the state. That news shocked many people, including Lianlian. She wondered if anyone had known she was an enemy of the state.

Jun said, "Some people I know had their suspicions about her. But who knows exactly what happened? The situation proves to be complicated. I did not let you children get involved earlier to avoid you accidentally repeating something you heard to others. That might expose us to those with evil intentions who might report us."

Over the next several years, under the paramount leader Deng Xiaoping, several campaigns corrected mistakes made during the Cultural Revolution. There were both explicit and implicit critiques of some of Mao's policies and conduct, which shocked Lianlian further. More than anything, she was confused.

Why are certain things correct at one time and wrong at another? Who should judge what's right and what's wrong? Who should we believe and trust? Maybe the world is a lot more complex than I thought. Maybe I should just keep my eyes open and quietly observe.

That was her takeaway.

25

LOST VIOLIN

T eacher Wu was the head music teacher at the junior high
school.

Music education in the 1970s involved learning and reciting the
Cultural Revolution songs and dances (later known as Red Songs
and Red Dances). Teacher Wu wanted to expand on that by offering
an extra musical education opportunity. He started by experiment-
ing with teaching various string instruments to a select group of
students.

Teacher Wu was in his forties. He wore a pair of glasses with
lenses as thick as the bottom of a glass cup and temples affixed to the
frame with white tape. He spoke little, but when he did, everyone
listened. There was something about him that commanded dignity
and respect. When he was to conduct a choir, he took his time to
limp toward the podium, his upper body shifting from one side to
the other—a childhood disease had affected his left leg. Everyone
stared at him but waited patiently for him to be ready.

Lianlian was 13 and in her first year of junior high. The early
spring weather was still chilly. One day, Teacher Tuan told her to
report to Teacher Wu's office after school. Lianlian knocked on

Teacher Wu's office door, wondering if she had done something wrong or inappropriate because someone always singled her out.

Teacher Wu opened the door, looking out through his thick lenses, his face looking serious as usual.

"I'm from Class 13. Teacher Tuan said I should report to you," Lianlian said in a shaky voice.

Teacher Wu's expression grew warmer, with a slight smile that Lianlian had never seen.

"Ah, yes. Is your name Zhou Lianlian? Come on in." He stepped aside and let Lianlian enter the room.

Three other girls were in the office, occupying three of the four chairs in front of a long table. Lianlian recognized they were from other classes in the same cohort. She sat in the empty chair.

"Good, you're all here." Teacher Wu stood in front of the table and nodded to everyone warmly.

"Your homeroom teachers recommended you to me because you are outstanding students." He scanned them as if to gain confirmation.

Lianlian let out a silent sigh of relief.

"I'm forming a music team to learn string instruments. You will each learn a particular instrument, and we'll have lessons in school—but you must practice daily at home. Are you interested?"

There was silence. The girls looked at each other.

This was new to Lianlian on several levels. First, Teacher Wu had asked the students if they were interested. Very often, students or children were told what to do, regardless of whether they were interested. Second, this seemed to be an opportunity falling from the sky. Learning musical instruments? Lianlian couldn't remember any students bragging about knowing how to play musical instruments. She had wanted to learn to play instruments when she and her sister stayed at her uncle's home because her uncle Xi-Dan had an extensive collection. But that never happened. Plus, Teacher Wu said the four of them were outstanding students who'd been recommended by their homeroom teachers. That meant this was a recognition, a distinctive one, because among hundreds of students in her cohort, these were the only four recommended.

Lianlian looked at the girls and Teacher Wu, then raised her hand.

"Yes, Lianlian?"

"I'm very interested," said Lianlian.

The other three girls looked at each other and raised their hands as well.

"I'm very interested, too," they each said.

"Very good. Can you promise to practice daily?"

"Yes," Lianlian nodded.

"Yes," the other girls replied and nodded.

"Very good. We will start today. Let me show you the instruments."

Teacher Wu limped toward a tall cabinet and opened the doors. Inside it, there were many instruments on multiple shelves.

"These are the school's instruments, and I am the gatekeeper. Come over, take these to the table."

The girls took what he passed to them and put the instruments on the long table.

All four instruments were stringed instruments with fingerboards. The violin and the erhu required a bow. The pipa or lute (pear-shaped) and the sanxian (three-stringed) were played with either fingers or a plectrum, similar to a guitar.

Teacher Wu tuned them one by one. Although the instruments looked old and had cracked paint, they filled the office with loud, crisp, delicious sounds.

"Now, let me look at your hands."

He examined each girl's hands.

"Lianlian, you take the violin. You have big hands, and the two little fingers of your left hand are straight."

So, one must have big hands and straight fingers to play the violin!

That notion stayed with Lianlian for a long time. She was glad she had inherited her mom's big hands.

Teacher Wu explained each instrument's features and showed how to play a simple sound. Then he assigned homework to the girls.

"Record your daily practice in this workbook." He passed a thin booklet to the girls. Inside the booklet, there were places to fill in the date, the task, and repetition numbers.

The four girls stayed after school every day. Teacher Wu taught them together and separately. They took their instruments home to practice.

Lianlian felt special and privileged. She was proud, grateful, and took the opportunity seriously. She was quick to study in lessons and practiced diligently at home.

Shanshan tolerated the horrific sound of Lianlian's practice sessions. On the days of violin lessons, she volunteered to carry the violin for Lianlian. In return, Lianlian let Shanshan play the violin for a few minutes.

Jun was proud and happy for Lianlian, too. She had sensed something more promising with this opportunity. With so many people, everyone tried to find a niche talent or skill to help them stand out. It had frustrated Jun that she could not offer more opportunities for her girls. The violin might open the door for Lianlian to develop special skills to secure a job opportunity in the future, such as joining an orchestra.

White spots and cracks marred the violin case. Jun made a cover out of an old, thick sofa wrap. The cover looked great and even had a handle.

Lianlian made steady progress. That pleased Shanshan and Jun because the sound from her practicing improved and became tolerable.

That also impressed Teacher Wu. He gave her more pointers during her lessons to match her progress, and he trusted her to master the new music before the next lesson.

Four months later, the violin disappeared.

Jun's house experienced three break-ins within two years. Although burglaries happened during that time in China, it was highly unusual for them to occur in this neighborhood. Jun's home was in the middle of a building. Targeting her made little sense, except for the fact that hers was the only home without a man living there.

Peculiarities made Jun and her friends speculate that someone had targeted her for reasons other than possessions, since she had few. For example, during one break-in, the burglar(s) poured water on the bedding and messed up the furniture but stole nothing. During the third break-in, they took the violin and new fabric Jun had just bought to make shirts for the girls.

The police took a detailed report of the third break-in. They interviewed the neighbors. Ge Meng, the boy two houses away, was sick at home that day. He reported that during a visit to the public bathroom, he saw two young men walking in the hallway, their faces covered halfway by scarves. He had thought the strangers might have gotten lost because the hallway was not a public path. His description of the two young men's ages, body shapes, and heights made Jun believe they were Uncle Shorty and Uncle Naughty.

Lianlian's head filled with boiling blood, and her heart sank low.

Why did they do this? What did they want from us? It has been over ten years since they beat Mom. Haven't they done enough damage? Such break-ins and disrupting our lives only strengthen one thing: I will never accept those bastards or their families as mine!

Because of a lack of further evidence, the police could not proceed further, and the case went cold. The violin was never found, and the dream of playing the violin vanished. Lianlian was heartbroken at losing the opportunity. But her wish for music and music education only became stronger.

Maybe not now. But someday in the future.

26

CUSTODY PROPOSAL

In 1977, Lianlian turned 14 and was one year from graduating junior high. Jun worried about the girls' future.

The government policy was that a household could have only one child living in the city. The rest of the children had to go to the countryside after graduating from school to receive continued education from peasants and other working classes.

This Down-to-the-Countryside Movement called for young people to do manual labor and live among farmers. These re-educated young people mostly experienced negative consequences: they lived in poor conditions, performed heavy physical work, and often faced emotional, physical, or sexual abuse. Several factors might draw these young people back to the city: their parents' early retirement, serious family health issues, or family connections to job openings. No one knew how many educated young people were still in the countryside. In 1976 alone, more than one and a half million young people were sent to the countryside nationwide. Over the years, these young people earned the labels of "the Sent-Down Youth" or "the Lost Generation."

Jun couldn't bear the idea of having either of her girls sent to the countryside. One approach to resolving this involved asserting that each child came from a single-child family.

Before the fall semester began, she contacted Bin-Kai. He remained unmarried, although he was dating. There were no children in his household.

"Fine. I want Shanshan," Bin-Kai clearly stated his preference. He had always sensed a strong connection with Shanshan, but not so much with Lianlian.

Jun had a different plan. Of the two girls, Lianlian showed more maturity and emotional connection with Jun, so losing Lianlian to her father was less likely. Jun wasn't sure the same would be true for Shanshan.

Jun persuaded Bin-Kai to take Lianlian instead. "Lianlian is older and more mature. She can take care of herself. You won't have to worry too much about her."

"I don't mind Shanshan being young," responded Bin-Kai. He recalled how annoyed, even furious, he had been when Jun had shown a firm opinion. For that reason alone, he didn't want her to get what she wanted this time.

"Take Lianlian. I am suggesting this for your sake. You're dating, and you have little childcare experience. Lianlian does not need your attention or care. You don't want to have Shanshan; she will jeopardize your new relationship and lifestyle."

"What did you say? I have little experience with raising children? I'll show you I can do a much better job than you if you send Shanshan to me. YOU think about it."

The conversation resulted in a standoff.

"Mom, is something wrong?" Lianlian asked. She'd noticed her mom had seemed worried for days.

"You're about to start the last year of junior high school. You know what will happen after that—I don't want you to go to the countryside."

"One of us has to go, just like the neighbor kids and the siblings of my classmates."

"Not if one of you goes to live with your father. We can tap into the single-child household policy."

Lianlian's body tensed. Living with Father? A chill ran down her spine.

"Who? Me or Shanshan?" she asked with a shaky voice.

"I am hoping you will go." Jun ran through her head what other arguments she could use to convince Bin-Kai. She didn't notice the expression on Lianlian's face and didn't explain her reasons.

Jun's answer shocked Lianlian.

Why does Mom want me to go? Shanshan has a much better relationship with Father. Does this mean Mom doesn't care that much about me anymore? But she reached out to Father to prevent either of us from going to the countryside. She's doing this to protect me from going to the countryside.

Lianlian wanted to ask why, but Jun's absentmindedness intimidated her. She didn't want to upset her mother, as if she were challenging her.

Two weeks later, Jun came home and lost her temper over every tiny little thing. Throughout the evening, the girls were walking on eggshells.

"Have you done your math homework yet?" Jun suddenly asked Shanshan. She didn't normally check the girls' homework.

"Umm. I did most of it." Shanshan said sheepishly.

"You'd better listen to me. How many times have I told you to finish your daily math homework?"

"I'm still doing it. I can finish it before bedtime," Shanshan whispered.

"You'd better, or your father may beat you. He's very good with math and very proud of his math skills."

Lianlian and Shanshan looked at each other with puzzled faces. Since when did Bin-Kai care about their math or any school subject?

"Damn it. Why does he want Shanshan and only Shanshan?" Jun blurted out. She had no one else to discuss the matter with, and she had been so frustrated dealing with Bin-Kai.

The room was quiet. Then, Shanshan's sobs filled the air.

"Mom, I'll do my best on my homework. I'll do any house chore you give me. Please don't send me to Father. Please don't make me leave my sister," Shanshan pled.

Lianlian looked at her mom, then Shanshan, then back at her mother. Her head spun with thoughts.

Poor Shanshan. What a horrible life she would have if she lived with Father! But wait, Mom didn't show any sign that she would send Shanshan. Mom was frustrated because Father wants someone she doesn't want to give. They both want Shanshan. And neither of them wants me. No one wants me! Neither of my parents wants me!

Lianlian's body froze. She wanted to shake her head as if to shake off the unwanted thoughts, but she couldn't. The realization that she was unwanted paralyzed her.

Doing household chores became more obligatory than voluntary. In the past, she'd taken pride in helping her mother and the household. Now, housework had lost its appeal.

The situation grew worse. Jun had lost her temper more times than usual because Bin-Kai argued with her every time she approached him. He even threatened to withdraw his agreement to take one child in.

Jun was unhappy at home because the girls didn't seem to support her intention to save them from having miserable lives in the countryside. Rather than seeing them as intimidated or depressed, she believed they were naughty or lacked understanding. She amplified any small imperfection in the girls' work. She continued to lecture Shanshan about her math homework, about not being on time to feed the chickens, and about not collecting eggs. Upon seeing Lianlian's lack of effort in doing household chores, she yelled at her. She had hardly ever shouted at Lianlian. To Lianlian, it was yet another confirmation that Mom didn't want her anymore.

In the past, Shanshan had shared what happened at home with outsiders. Those stories then became something others used in order to bully or laugh at them. Because of that, Lianlian had promised herself she would share nothing bad at home with outsiders. Now she wanted to talk to someone, but she didn't have anyone to talk to. Over the years, Lianlian had learned she shouldn't reveal all her emotions to her little sister because Shanshan needed protection. Plus, in the current situation, Shanshan was involved.

One day after school, as usual, Lianlian walked home with her best friend Li Ling. They acted as each other's shadows at school.

Both studied hard and cared less about socializing with others. Both were very good at math. When Teacher Tuan asked math questions in class, very often they'd both raise their hands, sometimes at the same time. When one of them was struggling, it was likely the other was struggling, too. Teacher Tuan often mentioned their names together as if they were one unit. He frequently used their homework solutions in class discussions.

Despite being her best friend, Li Ling knew little about Lianlian's life outside of school. For the first time, Lianlian broke her promise and said to Li Ling, "Things aren't right at home. I might not attend school for much longer."

"What do you mean?"

"I have to leave home. My mom doesn't want me anymore."

"What? Did you upset her? Is she kicking you out of the house?"

"I did nothing wrong. But she wants me to go to my father's home."

Li Ling knew that Lianlian's parents had divorced. She had a feeling that Lianlian's father was not a good person because he never showed up at school, and she'd hardly ever heard Lianlian mention him.

"You don't want to go, right?"

"No. But I need to go somewhere. Maybe I can go to my second uncle's. My sister and I have spent almost a year at his house in the past. His name is Xi-Dan."

"Does he have children?"

"Yes, three. Umm. He can't afford another child." She recalled that at his home, they'd barely had enough food, even though Jun provided financial support.

"Do you have other relatives?"

"My aunt Xia. She likes me. I like her too. She has three boys and always wanted a girl."

"That will work out great! But how do you get there? Does she live far away?"

"Yes, in Sichuan Province."

Both girls were quiet, figuring out how to get there. It would be a long way — by train, then by bus, with several transfers.

Lianlian said goodbye to Li Ling, determined to go to her aunt's place. She imagined how happy Xia would be when she saw Lianlian.

Wait. If Mom finds out, she'll be upset with my aunt. And my aunt will have to send me back. Plus, my aunt has three children, all younger than me. They face the same issue of having to go to the countryside.

The next day, Lianlian told Li Ling her thoughts, and Li Ling agreed.

"Maybe it's best you just go to your father's. Once you graduate from school, you can find a job and leave him."

"But he doesn't want me—he wants Shanshan." Her sadness was written all over her face.

That alarmed Li Ling. She stared at Lianlian but couldn't find anything to say.

The following week was blurry.

Jun had to get her up in the morning. Shanshan had to remind her they were late for school. She dragged herself home after school and forced herself to prepare dinner so that her mother wouldn't get mad. In the evenings, she stared at her homework booklets but could not finish them.

The next several days, she didn't submit her homework. First, she missed homework in all subjects except math. Then she missed math homework too. Teacher Tuan called on her in class because she hadn't raised her hand for days. But she could not answer his question.

Every morning, she forced herself to get up, wash her face and brush her teeth because Shanshan was waiting for her so they could go to school together.

She ate, but she didn't feel hungry. She walked, but didn't know where she was going. She looked in front of her but saw nothing. Darkness followed her everywhere.

One day on the radio, there was news about a young boy being killed while crossing a railroad track.

"Did you hear that? A boy was killed on the train tracks. Right here at the station close to home!" Shanshan repeated the news.

Lianlian stared at Shanshan. "Train station? Close to home?"

"Yeah. Remember, we got in from that spot? I tore my shirt when we visited it."

Right. I remember, Lianlian thought, making a mental note.

The following week, for two days in a row, Lianlian visited the train station. She got in just like she had done with Shanshan when they were in elementary school, not long after they'd moved to the new home.

On the first day, she checked out the entry and walked along the track. No one approached her.

On the second day, just when she planned to walk longer than the first day, someone called to her from behind.

"Hey, young lady, stay right where you are!"

Lianlian stopped and turned around. A worker walked fast toward her. He was wearing a protective helmet and holding a big wrench.

"What are you doing here?" he asked.

Lianlian thought he was very tall, almost as tall as her father, but stockier. Despite his fast steps and tall and bulky figure, she didn't find him intimidating.

"Just walking."

"How did you get in here? No one should be in this area except the workers—it's too dangerous." His voice was calm yet concerned.

Lianlian paused. She didn't want to point out the gap in the fence. If they fixed it, she wouldn't be able to come back.

"That gate." She turned around and pointed. Her heart jumped fast, and her face blushed. She'd just lied.

"What's your name?" The worker asked. His soft voice made Lianlian feel as if she were standing in the sun on a cold winter day.

Lianlian hesitated. She didn't easily give out her name. But something about the worker made her lower her guard.

"Zhou Lianlian. My name is Zhou Lianlian."

"Zhou Lianlian, which school do you go to? Which grade?"

Lianlian couldn't take her eyes away from his face. She wished her father would look at her this way and talk to her in this voice. *Oh, well. He never did and never will.* Taking a deep breath, she answered, "Hohhot 2nd Middle School. I just started the third year."

"That's about 25 minutes away from here. Where do you live?"

Lianlian became alert. Regardless of how she felt about this worker, she didn't want to tell him where her home was.

"About five minutes from here. I... I used to come here to watch the trains with my sister."

She wanted to leave now. She turned around and took a step.

"You should go home now. This is not a place for members of the public. Last week's accident caused us a lot of grief. Poor boy. He would still be alive if he hadn't come here to play with his buddy. You must have heard the accident?"

Lianlian nodded. That is why she was here. She'd wanted to check it out. Now she wanted to get out of here as quickly as possible.

"Sorry to cause you concern. I was just walking and thinking. I'll go home now."

"Good. Don't come back again. Let me lead you to the gate."

The worker directed Lianlian to the large gate for luggage carts.

As Lianlian walked home, her head was wild.

It was definitely possible—if she just closed her eyes while walking around the track, it could be a quick and easy solution to end her family's troubles. She could make it look like an accident.

The idea became more vivid and plausible. Somehow, Lianlian felt relieved. She was not sad or scared anymore. It was better than imagining living with either of her parents.

Li Ling became suspicious when she saw Lianlian at school.

"Has something changed?" she inquired.

"No, but I've found a solution. I'll show you today."

After school, they walked to the railroad station. They got in through a narrow opening next to a shed, and there they were, right in front of the tracks.

"What? You can't do that!" Li Ling cried.

"It's not bad. Really. I bet it'll be better than any day I'd have to live," Lianlian declared.

"But, but..."

Li Ling continued to cry.

"Don't worry. I won't do it now. I'll wait until I have no other choice, no other place to go."

Li Ling's eyes brightened.

"Wait! Don't do it at all. What if we don't have go to the countryside anymore? What if your mom changes her mind?"

Lianlian thought for a long while. She hadn't planned to disappear right away. What if her mother changed her mind? What if another opportunity existed that she had not known yet? Looking back, the train track idea was quite naïve. She had endured her father's cruelty when she was young. Her mother's bad temper was painful to deal with, but she had borne it. There might be a better way for her to get out of the situation. She just needed to find out.

Examining Li Ling's face, Lianlian felt guilty. Her thoughts and actions had troubled her best friend. What would have happened to her mother and her sister if she had done anything horrible?

"Sorry I have concerned you. My idea was childish. I won't do it. This can't be the only way to solve the problem. There must be other ways that I don't know yet. But please don't tell anyone about this idea. No need to alarm anyone. I only entrusted it to you."

Li Ling did not tell anyone. And there was no need to tell anyone.

PART III

FAMILY BECOMING TWO. 1977–1980

27

GLIMPSE OF A FUTURE

First came the whispers through the grapevine. Then came the official announcement in 1977, one year after the Cultural Revolution ended.

The government announced competence-based entrance exams for vocational schools and colleges. This was a tremendous change from the decades-long practice of admitting only politically and socially promising youngsters. Optimism spread among young people and their families as regular citizens gained access to colleges or vocational schools regardless of socioeconomic status. Getting into college or vocational schools eliminated the need to go to the countryside.

Suddenly, studying gained life-and-death importance. Everyone admired outstanding students.

Lianlian met more smiling faces from her classmates and received more attention from her teachers. She never liked to be noticed, but she was singled out more often than before, and in positive ways. She didn't know how to feel about the change. These positive moments correlated with her excellent academic performance.

As the end of junior high school approached, students filled out a form for their post-graduation plans.

Lianlian thought her best opportunity would be to attend a vocational school. Such schools provided tuition and living costs, which could make her independent. Plus, they required students to live in the dormitories, a perfect way for her to stay away from both of her parents.

Her plan shocked Teacher Tuan when he read her form.

At the parent-teacher conference, Teacher Tuan spoke with conviction and passion.

"This is a waste of her talent and her entire life. She should go to high school, then college, to have a bright future!" He tried to control his tone as he spoke to Jun. Jun didn't know what he was referring to. After Teacher Tuan explained, she was silent for a long time. It troubled her she had never explained to Lianlian the reason for wanting to send her to her father. Her lifelong regret was attending vocational school—a fact Lianlian understood from her many mentions.

My goodness, how much hurt Lianlian must have endured. I should have been more sensitive and shown her my love. I need to communicate with her.

"Lianlian, I should have told you the reason. I thought you understood. It was not because I loved you less. You should know that I love you and care about your future. I just trusted you more than I trusted your sister. That was the reason I wanted to send you to live with your father."

Lianlian looked at her mom. Part of her believed in her mom, and part of her still hurt.

Teacher Tuan asked Jun, "Now, do you agree Lianlian should switch her plan to attending high school?"

"Of course! I'll help her enter college, the best college in the entire country."

Jun was excited and energized. She might not have earned a college degree herself, but now she saw hope for Lianlian, whose academic track record filled her with unshakeable certainty about her future success. Her mind ran wild planning what to do to help Lianlian. Her attention turned to her ex-husband.

Zhou Bin-Kai, I don't need your help anymore. The children can build their own futures. You will miss out on their growth!

Lianlian was relieved. She wouldn't have to live with her father. She received her mother's explanation and an apology—which surprised her, in a good way. Grown-ups never apologized to their children. Lianlian was beyond glad when her home life became normal again, even better than normal. She and Shanshan continued to share household chores. But she noticed her mom eased up on their workload, especially Lianlian's. She sensed Jun envisioned grand aspirations for her.

Nervousness hit Lianlian, too. From everything she'd heard on the radio, from Teacher Tuan at school, and from her mom at home, she needed to build her future. She'd never considered the future much, but it remained unavoidable.

What is the future? A place to live? A job to earn money? A way of living? Can I build one for myself? What if I fail? Can't I just do what I enjoy doing now and worry about my so-called future later? I'm only 14.

28

FAST CHANGING NATION

1977 was the year Lianlian saw significant changes in public places and at home—positive changes. The most striking change involved China opening to international collaboration with ideas, experiences, trade, and business growth.

Gradually, people heard the stories of those who traveled abroad.

The most desirable perk for them was the privilege of purchasing two items from a luxury goods list, including TVs, washing machines, refrigerators, watches, and stereos. No one else could get them without the correct allowance tickets, even if they possessed ample money. Upon returning home, these lucky workers paid a visit to the Overseas Service Department to pick up the requested items. Although there were items made in China, the most desirable items were imported, as there was a stereotypical belief that they were better. People heard of a string of countries where the best items were manufactured, such as Switzerland, Sweden, Japan, and Germany.

For people who could not go abroad and get the fancy foreign item allowances, there were other goods to buy. More goods appeared in the department stores controlled by the government, and that's where everyone got items for everyday life.

Jun wanted to buy a new sewing machine, something she'd long desired and had been saving for. In the past, very few sewing machines were available. People had told each other, "Tomorrow morning, this department store will issue tickets for the next bunch of sewing machines." Those interested would spend the night in line, get a ticket in the morning if they were lucky, and wait to be notified to buy, usually months later. Jun attended one of those overnight lineups and didn't get a ticket, because the "back-door" swallowed the tickets.

This time, Jun was delighted when a friend shared that the department store now had many units that were available without tickets. She purchased one at once. A sewing machine boosted the process of making clothes, bedding, and even shoe pads.

"Mom, can I learn to use the sewing machine?" Lianlian asked after seeing Jun use it several times. The sound coming from the machine was soothing and hopeful.

"Sure. You can practice on straight lines and smooth curves by sewing shoe pads." Jun gladly showed Lianlian how to do it.

These pads provided warmth and filled up the extra space in the shoes Jun made for the girls. Sewing bed sheets was another way to practice. This was not child's play of making doll clothes like she and Shanshan had once done. This time, her mom used Lianlian's finished products. She felt great pride and a sense of being grown up and important.

On the sides of main roads, especially closer to the department stores, farmers from nearby towns would lay blankets or cardboard on the ground to sell fresh produce or homemade crafts. Individuals could never normally sell goods before this—people had always bought items from government-controlled stores.

But now people sold ready-to-eat homemade food, such as pancakes or tea-boiled eggs. An old lady with a basket of tea-boiled eggs came to the campus gate every day during the lunch break. These tea-boiled eggs had dark shells, and the eggs inside were hard and marble-looking because of the soy sauce and tea used during the hour-long boiling. They were the same kind most families could make. But students loved the idea of spending a few pennies to get one, and the eggs were warmer and tastier. Later, one could find steamed buns and even candy. Those staying during the lunch breaks because of the greater distance from their homes were not the only students buying such goodies.

One day, the girls took the government-issued allowance tickets to go shopping. Since most counters had long lines, they each had to buy separate items at separate counters. Shanshan was inside the grocery store to buy pork. Lianlian stayed outside the store to buy tofu. Before she got to the front, the clerk announced that tofu was gone for the day and people would have to come the next day.

Just then, a middle-aged man put two large baskets near the line.

"Tofu—tofu—freshly made tofu—" he sang out melodically.

"How much?" one man asked. Others looked on with suspicion.

"Same price as the store's tofu," the seller answered.

The line curved toward the baskets at once. The man sold everything in a matter of minutes.

Lianlian was lucky to get the two cakes of tofu she'd planned to buy. She told her mom what happened and showed her the allowance tickets that she hadn't used.

"Maybe we can throw these tickets away now?"

"Not yet, just in case. But it shows Deng's white and black cat is working."

Jun was referring to the famous statement by Deng Xiaoping: "No matter white or black, a cat is a good cat if it catches a mouse." The statement encouraged people to focus on practical values instead of considering a family's class, which was intensified during the Cultural Revolution. It influenced polices that allowed individuals to offer goods and services. The economy expanded at lightning speed. Because of the increased abundance of supplies, the government's control of essential resources became unnecessary.

The next big item Jun wanted to buy was a new bike. As the primary personal transportation method, bikes had been in high demand and short supply. Similar to a sewing machine, one had needed to wait in line.

Bin-Kai had made a 26-inch green bike in the spring of 1973. Instead of a straight bar between the handlebar and the rider's seat, it had featured a downward-sloping bar. People called this kind of bikes a lady's bike because it allowed women to ride it while wearing skirts. Having the backseat meant she could carry only one more person. On the streets, it was common to see three people on a bike—the front bar and the backseat were each for a passenger. Large bikes had the capacity for two small children on the front bar.

He had intended it to be a gift to his wife. After the divorce in 1973, he had left the small bike parked in his yard and occasionally lent it to his neighbors. It was too small for his 183 cm (6 feet) frame. Plus, he had another bike to use.

From their new home, Jun walked 15 minutes to work, and it took 20 minutes for Shanshan and Lianlian to walk to school. When they had to buy heavy items such as bags of flour or rice, Jun borrowed a bike from a colleague or friend. When the girls got bags of vegetables from the market for the chickens, they carried them in their hands or on their shoulders.

In 1975, two years after the divorce and moving to the new home, Jun had asked Bin-Kai if the girls could have the small bike to use for middle school. Bin-Kai agreed. By that time, the bike had seen better days. The inner tubes, after being patched repeatedly, leaked air. To avoid patching costs, the girls had regularly pumped them up. Chipped paint exposed rust in several areas. Yet, the bike had given them the joy of riding to school and anywhere else they had to go. Usually, Lianlian rode, and Shanshan sat in the back. It had become a tremendous help when they carried bags of goods home. But that bike had given out entirely.

Jun's new bike represented a tremendous improvement. With a standard 28-inch, steady frame, it had a straight front bar and was a shiny black. It was not just a new bike; it was a new bike with a brand name, which made Jun proud. At night, Jun told the girls to put the new bike in their main room, not in the yard, where the small green bike had been located.

One day, Shanshan casually remarked during dinner.

"One of my classmates said her family got a large black-and-white TV. Another classmate said her family got a color TV. None of their parents traveled overseas."

Lianlian recalled her amazement when she and Shanshan had first viewed television four years prior. In the neighborhood of their new home, there was an open space in the adjoining neighborhood. Someone had arranged a 9-inch black-and-white TV on the windowsill of a house. Lianlian and Shanshan had sat on the ground behind the younger kids. The grownups had sat on their stools and benches behind the children. More people stood at the back. People waited patiently for the TV to come on. There must have been more than 30 people that evening. Chatting and murmuring stopped at once when signals showed on the TV. After random images and flashes, news briefs appeared on the screen: the countryside, factories, army soldiers, and Chairman Mao.

Witnessing vivid scenery and images of people walking and talking in a box proved unbelievable. Lianlian's eyes were fixed on the screen, and she forgot to breathe. Shanshan squeezed her hand, she let out a long exhale, and Shanshan did the same. When the program was over and there was no more picture on the screen, many people chatted excitedly. Like the girls, they felt awe.

The girls discussed it for days and told Jun the details they saw on TV. They returned to that place many more times. Sadly, the person who owned that TV soon stopped sharing it with the neighborhood.

After dinner, Jun responded to Shanshan's comments on TV.

"It's important for you two to focus on studying. A TV will distract. If any programs are worth watching, we can go to my office."

The conference room at Jun's workplace had a large color TV. Lianlian knew her mom must be tight on money, too.

Not having a TV at home did not prevent them from watching fun TV programs. Jun took the girls to her office to watch every showing of the China Women's National Volleyball Team.

The volleyball team dominated the news—on the radio, in the newspaper, and on TV. Newly formed in 1976 and coached by Yuan Weimin, the team of young women reached higher international rankings than before the Cultural Revolution. Right off the bat, the team ranked Number 4 in the World Cup in 1977.

The coach and team members became everyone's favorites. People thought of them as family members. Before every match, regardless of level or region, Jun reminded Lianlian and Shanshan to complete their homework and chores. Then she took them to her office to watch the game on a big color TV.

The volleyball team continued as a superpower in the following. They reached Number 6 in the World Championship in 1978, and Number 2 in the Asian Games. Then later, in 1979, they ranked number one at the Asia Volleyball Championship, beating the dominant Japanese national team.

The Women's National Volleyball Team set the tone for the entire country and motivated everyone to aim high. The slogan "Breaking out of Asia and Reaching the Globe" applied not only to the volleyball team but to every facet of life in China.

For the first time, at 14, Lianlian internalized the existence of other countries and the improving image of China globally. Every mention of the volleyball team or other positive world news about China increased Lianlian's pride in being Chinese.

29

EDUCATION REFORM

J un rushed home from work.

"Look! This is today's newspaper—I borrowed it from the office."

Lianlian and Shanshan stopped preparing dinner and bent their heads over the newspaper on the table.

China's higher education department was announcing a new classification system for all existing colleges and universities. The categories included: National Key Universities, National Non-Key Universities, Provincial Key Universities, and Provincial Non-Key Universities. Within each category, there were multiple levels, such as Tier 1 and Tier 2.

Lianlian turned to her mother's excited face. "What does this mean?"

"It means for those with top performance, they can go to the top, most prestigious universities. They will receive more respect—this will define a person's class now, instead of the old class system that prioritized a family's background."

Jun took a deep breath and let it out with a loud noise. "Finally!"

Lianlian sensed the significance of the news from Jun's reaction.

The end of 1977 marked a monumental shift across the entire country. Getting into college by studying hard and performing well became the primary goal for every household with youngsters.

Locally, at the regional/provincial and city levels, similar education reforms took place for junior and high schools.

Beginning with the 1978 cohort, students entering high schools must pass entry exams, which were the same across the entire Inner Mongolia Region. Those students with the top scores would gain admission to Regional Key High Schools in their respective home cities. The next bunch would go to City Key High Schools. The rest who passed the exams would attend other high schools that lacked a prestigious designation.

That year, Hohhot had over thirty high schools and only two Provincial Key High Schools: Hohhot No. 1 High School and Hohhot No. 2 High School.

Students also needed to choose a concentration in high school: science or liberal arts. Those students who struggled with math, physics, or chemistry would select the liberal arts.

The schools would put the very top science students into "Ace" classes so they could concentrate on preparing to enter National Key Universities. A high school's performance and prestige would be determined by the number and percentage of graduating students who'd been admitted by colleges and top-tier universities.

Both the junior and the high school curricula were adjusted—if a subject was not on the college entrance exam, it would be reduced or eliminated.

For junior high schoolers, their immediate goal was to enter a high school that could promise entrance to a college two years down the road. Nothing else mattered.

A few weeks after the announcement of Key High Schools, Lianlian's junior high class held a parent-teacher conference. Students did not attend the conference, but Teacher Tuan had asked Lianlian and Li Ling to help. Parents sat in their children's seats or stood along the walls.

Teacher Tuan presented his vision of taking the class forward. He laid out a few requirements and several suggestions for how parents could provide support at home.

"We all have to work on this goal together to make sure our children get into high schools—prestigious high schools." He paused and looked around. Many parents nodded eagerly.

"You should not ask them to cook or do household chores because they need to focus on studying."

Many more parents nodded.

"You should make sure they're healthy. Give them more meat, eggs, and nutritious food. Studying hard takes energy. They cannot do well if they're not feeling well."

More nods.

"We have some students who walk to school every day. Get them a bike or give them a ride to school so that they don't waste valuable time commuting," Teacher Tuan continued.

One parent raised a hand. "Is it possible for my daughter to bring her lunch and stay at school during the lunch hours so that she could take a nap here instead of commuting home?"

"I'll suggest to the principal that we keep the classroom open during lunchtime." The school normally locked the classrooms during the two-hour lunch break. Students would go home to have lunch and take a nap, then come back for afternoon classes.

Another parent piped up. "Will the students have extra classes to get additional help or learn additional materials?"

"For the moment, they should focus on the class materials given by their teachers. But just a heads up—I am developing additional math exercises and will provide them as bonus materials later."

Teacher Tuan then announced.

"If there are no further questions, you can look at the results of your child's last math exam. They're inside the drawer of your child's desk. The top two students' results are on the back tables." He pointed to the tables at the far end of the classroom where Lianlian and Li Ling stood.

There were noises and various facial expressions. Then, several parents rushed back to grab the best results and compare them to their own children's.

"Wait," one parent raised a paper in the air as if they'd found gold. "The answer to this last question is incorrect in this best exam result!"

"Bring it up here," Teacher Tuan gestured from the podium at the front of the classroom.

"I see. This is Zhou Lianlian's exam." He gestured to Lianlian. "Zhou Lianlian, come here and explain the answer you provided."

Lianlian was shocked. She did not feel prepared to stand in front of this many people, let alone speak.

Everyone turned their head, following her as she walked from the back of the room to the podium. Her heart was beating fast, and her face was burning. Not daring to look anywhere, she got to the blackboard, picked up some chalk with her shaky right hand, and wrote several symbols to show how she'd gotten the answer. She couldn't speak. Fortunately, she didn't need to—Teacher Tuan did the talking. He went through the entire process with a detailed annotation that made Lianlian's solution seem glamorous and brilliant. Her answer was correct, of course.

Everyone was quiet. Jun was beaming, her eyes sparkling.

"The other top student is Li Ling. Check out her result too. The two of them are not only good at math—they're good at all major subjects. Their parents must have done something great at home to support them." Teacher Tuan waved at Li Ling at the back. Everyone followed his hand and looked back. Li Ling's face turned bright red. She smiled awkwardly and could not decide where to put her hands.

"How does Zhou Lianlian study at home?" one mother asked Jun. "Do you tutor her?"

"Oh no. I hardly ever tutor her. She just likes to read and study and can easily get absorbed in what she reads. She has burned a cooking pot and a water pot in the past because she was reading," Jun shared with pride.

From that moment on, "Zhou Lianlian burned cooking pots while studying" became one of several stories Teacher Tuan passed on for generations. But the truth was that when those pots were burned, she hadn't been studying school subjects. She'd been reading a novel, and it had been a year before the education reform.

The college entrance exam was open to everyone regardless of their family class, personal background, income, gender, age, or prior education level. All that was needed for registration was the proof of citizenship, a document called Hu Kou.

On a chilly winter night in 1977, Jun asked Lianlian to add more coal to the stove to make the house warmer than usual. Four of her co-workers came after dinner. The three men and one woman ranged in age from mid-20s to mid-30s. They greeted Lianlian and Shanshan. Then, they moved the desk near the kang as Jun directed, with three people sitting on the kang and two in chairs. They pulled out pencils and pages of paper that had scribbles and writings. Jun pointed to some pages and answered their questions.

Lianlian recognized some materials they were discussing. Fascinated, after she had been observing for some time, she hesitantly recited the Pythagorean Theorem: "The square of the hypotenuse of a right triangle is equal to the sum of the squares of the other two sides." It was the problem they were stuck on.

All five of them raised their heads and stared at Lianlian, then checked the scratch paper in front of them.

"Have you learned this?" Jun asked.

"Yes, we started last week."

"Then, try to solve this." Jun pointed to a triangle on a piece of paper.

The problem was like some exercises by Teacher Tuan. It did not take Lianlian long to solve it.

"Lianlian! You should take the college entrance exam," the young lady exclaimed.

Lianlian blushed. "I'm still in junior high now. Um, so, you guys are preparing for the college entrance exam?"

"Yes. Your mom is so good at these math problems," the older man said. "She's been tutoring us at the office. I wish I remembered these materials from high school, but having two boys and a construction job wiped out my memory."

"I wish I'd learned more in high school," a young man followed. "But few of us did. We were busy being the Red Guards and touring around the country." Some Red Guards took the train and visited other cities during the Cultural Revolution. He must have been one of those.

"I didn't even go to high school," the other young man said. "My father retired early because of a work-related injury, so I've been in his position for the last few years. But I want to at least give this college thing a try, so that I have no regrets in the future."

"I just want to have a good job," said the young woman, "better than cleaning the hallways after coming back from the countryside."

"You're all doing the right thing to try. You'll regret it in the future if you don't," Jun said with a sigh. Lianlian knew her mom was speaking from experience.

"Do you think we still have time?" the young woman asked Jun. "The exam is in December, only a month away."

"Do what you can and try your best. There will never be enough time," Jun answered.

As they continued studying, Lianlian could not help but daydream.

These people are the lucky ones who already have jobs, yet they want to get into college. It seems getting into college is better than anything else, and one just needs to pass the entrance exam. There is no need for family connections, family background or class position, special skills or training, or even money. I never had training in gymnastics, swimming, calligraphy, etc., to make me special. But it doesn't matter now—having a bright future requires getting into college. I believe I can do that. I must study hard, study well, and get into a good high school, and then get into a college, a top university.

1977 was the only year that each province or region had its own different entrance exam subjects and test dates. Over five million people took part that year, yielding an acceptance rate of 4.74%, the lowest ever in the history of Chinese higher education.

That year's college cohort was named the "1977 Cohort," even though they started school in the spring of 1978.

Of the four young people Jun helped, only the older man received an acceptance to a college in Hohhot.

30

AIM FOR THE ACE

For the first time in 1978, students had to pass a region-wide entrance exam in order to get into a high school. There were no uniform preparation materials besides the standard textbooks that had been created many years ago. No one knew what questions might appear on the exam. Several teachers created extra materials for the students.

Teacher Tuan collected and compiled many math exercises. Copying machines didn't exist yet, so students had to hand-copy everything into their notebooks. To save students time, Teacher Tuan carved the math questions on a thin layer of foil-like paper that functioned as a stencil. Then, he used a roller and black ink to duplicate the content on paper. Teacher Tuan could only make a few copies before the stencil became flat, despite using a pointed metal pen to make deep marks. To make more copies, he had to rewrite the same content again onto another stencil. His right hand and wrist were soon covered with heavy wraps.

The effort showed promise. For many of the students who had the capacity for more material than what the textbooks offered, these extra exercises filled the gap and satisfied their need for learning.

Most importantly, their math exam results improved significantly. However, the loose papers of those bonus questions got lost easily.

Staplers were hard to find. Jun used sewing thread to make an X on the upper left corner of stacks of papers to make them stay together for Lianlian. Other parents did similar things, such as making two or three X marks on the left side. Yet the papers still tore easily. At a parent conference, one parent said he could bind a few booklets at his workplace. But when more booklets were needed, that parent could no longer help. Teacher Tuan explored local shops for a solution. It cost money to bind the loose papers into booklets with covers. He funded most of the cost and collected money from parents for the rest. Few families were rich, but parents rarely complained about paying for the booklets. Teachers had moderate salaries, no more than Jun's. Although Teacher Tuan's wife worked and earned a salary, a household with two young children was not prosperous. His actions were heroic. This early effort continued into the high school years and formed the foundation of his multi-volume, best-selling math reference books, which he would go on to publish.

Teacher Tuan was not the only teacher providing bonus materials. Other teachers did similar things, although not as systematically or on the same scale.

To improve, students needed to take simulated tests. Subject teachers worked together to generate questions and offer answers. The teachers announced students' results publicly in each class.

Gradually, a "ladder" of performance formed in Lianlian's class. Some students' names were almost always at the top, and some were always at the bottom. The top students got more attention from the teachers during self-study periods or bonus classes.

Five students consistently topped the math scores. Teacher Tuan spent more time with this group and provided more difficult bonus materials.

Slightly different groups were formed by the top students of other subjects, such as physics, chemistry, Chinese, and English.

The school encouraged students who were strong in English and Chinese to specialize in liberal arts to capitalize on their strengths.

Lianlian had been among the top groups consistently in all subjects except one, political studies. Maoism, Leninism, Marxism, etc., required more memorization than logical reasoning. However, the overall scores were the ones that determined college admission decisions. That was good news for Lianlian because she was often the top student in terms of the overall score.

Until that year, Lianlian had felt like an anonymous youngster. She had wanted to blend in and avoid the unwanted attention that was often caused by her family, rather than her own behavior. Almost overnight, those who could perform well in school became stars and the center of positive attention from teachers, students, and parents. Lianlian was one of them. She became the most-talked-about student. Everything about her was a mystery worth examining or scrutinizing. She was under watchful eyes all the time, some admiring, some curious, and many envious. When someone still tried to belittle her by mentioning, "Her parents are divorced," Teacher Tuan shouted back, "Focus on her being the top student, not on her family status."

This newfound attention brought mixed feelings. Lianlian wasn't comfortable being in the spotlight, regardless of the reason. But she sensed that what she did mattered. All she did was study and study hard. It was under her control to use her time to study. She didn't waste her time watching TV (in Jun's office or someone's home). She stopped reading novels she loved. Hanging out with friends was the last thing she wanted to do. She realized it made her feel good to concentrate on the challenges presented in each subject and to reach solutions after a struggle. She didn't care about competing with anyone else; she was competing with herself. This was a revelation to her.

The rest of the last year of junior high went by quickly.

Jun prepared nutritious meals and secured the girls' nap times every day. She also took over laundry and spent evenings at home sewing and knitting in case the girls had homework-related questions. She eliminated distractions from the girls' studies.

Shanshan's main household chore was being the primary caregiver for the chickens. Although not as internally driven as Lianlian, she did her homework at the opposite end of the desk when Lianlian studied. As a result, her school performance improved. She sensed that their mother put more hope in Lianlian than in her. She thought often: If I had no chores, like Lianlian, I could make Mom proud too.

Lianlian had more time at home to study in the evenings and on weekends. Unless she was sleeping, eating, or brushing her teeth, she was studying.

31

TYPICAL DAYS AT HIGH SCHOOL

The junior high school posted the high school entrance exam results on campus bulletin boards. This was the first time the boards had been used for something other than political or social announcements. They showed the ranking and cutoffs for various levels of high school entrance exams. Lianlian's name topped the list of the entire junior high school graduating cohort.

By fall, Lianlian learned she'd ranked third in her incoming class at Hohhot 2nd High School, one of the two provincial key high schools. The first and second-ranked students came from other junior high schools. Proximity to home became irrelevant. Many of the new classmates lived far away from school. Several had to live in rented places near campus to go to school.

The cohort formed 20 classes, each with 50 students. Classes #1 and #2 were for Mongolian students, where they'd learn Mongol as a foreign language instead of English. Classes #3 and #4 were Ace classes. Regular classes were from #5 to #17. Classes #19 and #20 were for liberal arts students.

Lianlian and thirteen of her classmates in her junior high school class made it to the first Ace class, Class #3. She was sad that her best friend, Li Ling, had moved to the south with her parents before high school started. To her great delight, Teacher Tuan was the homeroom teacher of Class #3.

There was no tuition at high school because the local government funded the public schools. Yet, Teacher Tuan asked the school to offer financial aid to Lianlian, explaining, "She is a top student coming from a family with limited income." The school agreed, and she became the first to receive financial aid during high school. It was not much money, but it was extremely helpful in buying basic school supplies such as pens, pencils, notebooks, and paper.

In the two-year high school, Lianlian found that hard work resulted in better performance, which earned her respect and recognition, and that boosted her pride and confidence.

The high school was a highly structured environment designed to fulfill everyone's goal of entering the best university upon graduation. Six days of the week, from early morning to evening, everyone's schedule was full.

On a typical day, Teacher Tuan demanded that everyone in his class do the morning run at 6:30 AM on the school playground. A self-study class started at 7:30 AM. Two subject classes followed that, with each lasting 50 minutes, and a 10-minute break. Next was the 30-minute-long morning recess. Every class in the entire high school division lined up and marched to the playground, where everyone followed instructions for standard stretching exercises. After recess and before lunch, everyone had one more subject.

The lunch break started at noon and lasted two hours. Most students went home to have lunch and take a nap, if possible. Those students who lived too far away brought their lunch and napped in the classroom by putting their heads on their desks.

Afternoon classes resumed at 2:00 PM. After two subjects, an open recess of 30 minutes took place, during which students were free to do any physical activities they wished. Two other subjects followed that. Physical education classes usually took place either right before lunch or in the afternoon. Around 6:00 PM, the students went home to have dinner.

From 8:00-10:00 PM, students returned to school for guided self-study, during which they completed their homework or projects. Although teachers did not have to visit, many of them did. They showed up, walked along the aisles, and answered questions. At 10:00 PM, students were free to go home for the day.

Sundays were weekend days, but not free. Various kinds of consulting and tutoring took place. For example, every Sunday morning, Teacher Tuan offered a bonus math class with extra materials or exercises. Although the class was optional, the pressure meant everyone treated it as mandatory.

One day during the afternoon recess period, Lianlian and three top female students wandered to the second floor of the physical education building. Although ping-pong, or table tennis, was a popular game, few people could find places to play because few families could afford the table or the space. During physical education classes, students had to wait in line for a turn and would be lucky to play one round before the class was over.

To the four girls' delight, the table was available on this day. They alternated playing singles and then doubles. They were having too much fun to notice the bell for the next class. The bell on that floor might not have been working. By the time they realized it was too quiet, they flew back to their classroom for the next class, which was a self-study class.

Breathing heavily after running across the campus and climbing up the stairs to the top floor, they reached the classroom door, which was wide open. Teacher Tuan was in the room, apparently bothered by the four empty seats. Lianlian knew at once they were in trouble.

Teacher Tuan's forehead was scrunched up like a bow tie. His glasses reached his nose tip, and he did not bother to push them back up. "Line up at the front. Explain where you've been. Why didn't you come back on time?"

The front of the classroom had a platform the width of the room and about one foot high.

Standing on the platform, Lianlian felt shamefully tall, even though she was one of the shortest girls in the class.

There was silence, and none of them dared to speak. Lianlian hung her head, and she stared at a spot on the ground in front of her.

Teacher Tuan targeted her. "Zhou Lianlian, where did you four go?"

Lianlian jumped. Blood rushed to her head, face, and arms. Keeping her head low and using a very low voice, she said,

"We were playing ping-pong and did not hear the bell."

"Did any of you have a watch?" Teacher Tuan asked.

Lianlian shook her head. None of them had watches.

There was a pause. It felt an hour long.

"In the future, be mindful of time during recess. Be aware of your surroundings if you have no watch. Now, go back to your seats." Teacher Tuan's voice softened. He waved his right hand as if to push the girls off the podium, then pushed up his glasses.

That was the most humiliating incident Lianlian experienced during high school.

No one ever dared to miss even one minute of class after that.

32

FRIENDSHIP AND FIRST CRUSH

On the first day of high school, Lianlian turned a corner toward her classroom and bumped into two girls who were chatting excitedly.

"Sorry," said Lianlian. Lowering her head out of habit, she walked to the side to pass.

"Oh, Hi! Zhou Lianlian!" A high-pitched voice stopped her. A dark-skinned, tall girl grinned at her as if she were Lianlian's long-lost best friend.

"Oh, hi," Lianlian gave a polite nod, but couldn't remember where they had met.

"Do you remember me? We were classmates in first grade. Our parents worked in the same institute." She continued to grin with pride.

That proud look and her dark skin reminded Lianlian of their childhood meeting. She was nicknamed Hei Guo Di, meaning the dark bottom of a cooking pot. She had once been a big bully because of her family's class—until the day Lianlian and Shanshan had taught her a lesson by treating her pigtails like a merry-go-round.

Lianlian examined Hei Guo Di's tall figure. Shoulder-length hair had replaced her long pigtails.

"Yes, I remember you." But she couldn't recall her real name.

"See? I told you I knew her!" She turned to the other girl, her pride jumping up another notch.

She turned to Lianlian again, as if to seize the moment. "We were just talking about you. Congratulations on being in Ace class #3."

"Thank you. Which class are you in?" asked Lianlian out of politeness. There was no reason to hold on to childhood dramas. Plus, she and her sister had won during that confrontation.

"Class #17. We both are." She pulled the other girl's arm as if that made it more acceptable.

"Good for you." She meant it. It was good to see childhood classmates make it to this high school. "See you."

"Yes! See you around!"

Lianlian had to mentally block out the high-pitched sound.

It just so happened that the Ace Class #3 had three girls whose names had the "Lian" sound in them, though they were different Chinese characters. The three of them would end up being best friends. For the sake of referring to them, let's call them Lian #1 (Zhou Lianlian), Lian #2 (Lu Jialian), and Lian #3 (Song Meilian).

It all started with Lianlian growing faster than most of her classmates.

Classroom seating arrangements were based on the height of the students. The classroom had four columns and six rows of tables, with two people seated at each table. Every Monday, the entire class moved one seat over in a clockwise direction. Each month, the seating arrangements were updated based on the lineups during recess.

"You are all growing. You should not sit in the same position, or you might develop bad posture," Teacher Tuan said to them.

At the start of high school, Lianlian had been among the shortest girls. Then, every two weeks, Lianlian would switch one position toward the taller end during recess.

At one point, Lianlian lined up next to Lian #2, Lu Jialian, and shared the same table with her. Lian #2 was in the middle section and stayed that way throughout high school. With a round face and a pair of smiling eyes, Lian #2 had a mellow and helpful personality. At first, Lianlian thought it might be because she was from another junior high school, so she was being humble and careful on the surface. Lianlian observed she was always ready to lend a hand. She helped with small things, such as sharing a pencil. She also helped with bigger tasks, like classroom chores or the bulletin board. Such activities required her to come in early, leave late, and sacrifice study time. Lianlian admired her altruism and felt at ease when they were together.

A few weeks into the semester, during the lineup for recess, Lianlian estimated her height and moved further down the line.

"I think you're shorter than me. Stay here," Lian #3 said, smiling brightly, with all her teeth showing. Tall and skinny, Song Meilian was about one-third from the end of the line. Her thick glasses made her eyes look very slim. Thinness was everywhere on her: skinny face, skinny arms, and skinny fingers.

Lianlian stood next to Lian #3 and slightly bent her legs, a gesture to match Lian #3's lighthearted attitude. They both laughed and became friends at once.

Naturally, they also got to share a table.

Lian #3 had a carefree personality. She laughed a lot without worrying about people looking at her. She was a little absent-minded and didn't have great situational awareness. There were many times during self-study classes when neighboring students shushed because Lian #3 was having a loud discussion with Lianlian or someone nearby. For some strange reason, instead of feeling embarrassment or annoyance, Lianlian felt liberation from Lian #3's behavior. She wished she could be as worry-free as Lian #3.

Both Lian #2 and Lian #3 were from the same junior high school, quite far away, and their homes were close to each other. The three Lians shared a part of the route going home. Since Lianlian didn't have a bike all the time, sometimes, Lian #2 and #3 would give Lianlian a ride on their bikes to the intersection where they'd separate.

"You're not intimidating after all!" Lian #3 exclaimed one day when the three of them were riding home. She was talking to Lianlian.

"No, not at all, as I told you already," Lian #2 chipped in.

"Intimidating? Me?"

"Oh, yes! You're the top student in most subjects. You have a serious expression on your face all the time, and you hardly ever smile or laugh," Lian #3 continued.

"Ha!—but you make me laugh! You both make me smile!" That might be the reason Lianlian befriended them—they made her feel safe.

The Lians walked to and from morning recess together. They spent time together during afternoon recess, too. Most importantly, they were among the top performers in the class. Lian #2 was an overall top performer in all subjects. Lian #3 was excellent in physics. Other girls joined them from time to time. But somehow, none of them stuck around long enough to become part of the "Lian" party.

The Three Lians became an item for the rest of high school. Others in their class and in other classes talked about them a lot.

Lianlian's first crush was in high school—or maybe it had started in junior high, without her realizing it. On the first day of the last semester of junior high school, Teacher Tuan brought in a transfer student. He was tall and slim, with a military haircut, a large pair of glasses on his pale face, neat clothing, and a bright smile. When he said "Hi" to the class, she felt he'd said it to her. She thought he looked very much like the young Elvis, based on a couple of pictures she'd seen, only with a more natural and less glamorous style. Elvis had a nickname in China—"Cat King." Lianlian hadn't heard his music, but she was aware of his popularity and pleasant looks. She immediately liked this boy's carefree style, his easy-going personality, his voice, how he moved, and his whole being, and she secretly named this lad her "Cat King." Besides noticing him in her peripheral vision more than she noticed other boys, that had been that, and nothing happened.

They both made it into the Ace class in high school. He was one of the six tallest boys in the class. The six of them always hung out together during breaks, recesses, or physical activities. As a group, they dominated space and attention. But Lianlian's "Cat King" always stood out because of his smile—it was sunshine to her. She rarely went a day without seeing his smile. The exception might have been the day of high school graduation photos, when everyone was stressed from studying for college exams.

It was a fresh sensation. Lianlian felt her heart beating fast, her breath growing heavy, her face burning whenever she laid eyes on him, or when she sensed him passing by her. So many times, she'd be so eager to find where he was and would feel satisfaction when she located him in a crowd. After she grew taller, she sat one row ahead of him and two tables away. That might have been a good thing, to keep her more focused on lessons during class.

In the last year of high school, they both became class officers. They interacted more than before but were still hardly ever alone together. Girls and boys did not talk to each other, or they would face accusations of being "not innocent." Once, he had to pass a document to her and explain it. Lianlian kept her eyes only on the paper because she was nervous. Then she noticed he could not hold the paper still, making it impossible for her to read it. His voice was shaking, and his words were unintelligible. She wondered if he was nervous too, and, if so, for what reason? It was difficult to make sense of that.

Lianlian didn't know if he had a crush on her or any other girls in the class. But she knew at least two other girls had a crush on him. One sat in front of Lianlian and constantly turned her head to look at him—it was so obvious. The other one always tried to find excuses to line up with him during recess, despite not being tall enough.

What if I am shamed by others like my junior high school classmate Lihua was? Plus, who knows if he likes me? Most importantly, what if he's good-looking but nasty inside, like Father? Studying is the most important thing. Nothing should interfere with it.

She hid this special sweet sensation inside her and carried on with her life.

33

SHANSHAN'S FALLING OUT

Lianlian's classmate Bobo ranked at the top in physics, but not in math and chemistry. On the exams, her overall scores were not as high as Lianlian's.

Bobo's younger sister was in the same class as Shanshan and shared the same table. At Shanshan's parent-teacher conference, Jun learned Shanshan had gotten into trouble by hitting Bobo's sister and making her nose bleed.

"What happened?" Jun asked Shanshan when they got home.

"She said she was better than me on the exam results. But I said my sister is better than her sister!" Shanshan recounted.

"And?" Jun asked.

"And after she said more stuff, I lost my temper."

"Don't compare sisters, compare yourself to your classmates," Jun snapped at Shanshan. She had not enjoyed a single parent-teacher conference about Shanshan.

Shanshan was conflicted. She was super proud of her big sister. Yet, she was jealous of Lianlian earning her mom's attention and everyone's praise. Shanshan wished her mom would pay more attention to her. These days, with everyone studying hard, her mother had put all her hope and effort into Lianlian. Whenever she came back from a teacher-parent conference, she'd be excited and happy if it had been about Lianlian, and concerned or even angry if it was about Shanshan. So far, Shanshan had not made her mom proud.

Shanshan tried to earn her mother's praise for doing housework.

"Mom, the chickens have been fed and locked up for the night," she said one day.

"You're supposed to do that every day. No need to tell me."

"Mom, I helped wash the vegetables. This saves time for you when cooking dinner."

"Next time, just use the time to study. I can wash before cooking."

"Mom, I'll do the dishes tonight."

"Okay. But make sure you finish homework before bedtime."

Shanshan grew lonely because Lianlian spent all her time studying and not playing with her. Shanshan missed those fond moments from their early days.

"Jie, can you go with me to the market today to gather veggies?" Shanshan tried it one day.

"Sorry, but I have too much homework to finish today. You go by yourself."

Jun's concern a few years earlier about easily losing Shanshan was not without validity.

One evening on a chilly winter weekend day in 1979, Lianlian, 15 and in her first year of high school, was doing homework, and Shanshan, 14, was playing with the radio. Jun was out visiting a friend after dinner.

The noise from the radio was loud and disturbing. Lianlian asked Shanshan to lower the volume. Shanshan didn't. After several rounds of asking and being ignored, Lianlian took one of the four batteries away. But Shanshan applied what she'd learned in physics and used a piece of metal to connect the batteries and continued to play the radio.

Jun came back from outside and saw the scene. She was annoyed.

"Why are you bothering Lianlian? Why play with the radio instead of doing your schoolwork? Turn off the radio!"

Shanshan turned off the radio with an I-don't-care expression on her face. That angered Jun. She blamed Shanshan for her poor performance at school, avoiding math homework, and having little chance of going to the same Tier 1 high school. Jun recalled Shanshan not doing enough household chores and not feeding the chickens on time. There had only been one time Shanshan didn't feed the chickens before dark, and they roamed in their chicken run, refusing to go to sleep. She had done it to see if her mom would pay attention to her.

Shanshan maintained her "whatever" face, which worried Lianlian. She knew that if Shanshan continued to do this, it would trigger her mother's temper, and something terrible would happen. And just as Lianlian feared, Jun hit Shanshan on the back of her head and slapped her face.

Shanshan opened the door and skipped outside without putting on her coat. Lianlian jumped up, fetched Shanshan's coat, and was about to go after her when Jun gestured to Lianlian to stop. "She'll be back."

Similar things had happened in the past, and Shanshan had always returned a few minutes later because it was freezing outside. But this time, she didn't come back even after a long time had passed.

Lianlian sat with her homework, but she could not concentrate.

Jun continued knitting a sweater, but Lianlian could tell she was not content.

The clock passed 11:00 PM, their usual bedtime.

Jun put the knitting aside and put on her coat, hat, scarf, and mittens. "I'm going out to find her. You go to bed because you need to get up early tomorrow for school."

Lianlian kept her clothes on and paced back and forth. She could not work on her homework and was not sleepy. She had a bad feeling: this time, Shanshan was acting differently, and that was not good.

Midnight came and went. Lianlian worried about her mom, too. *Where can Mom find Shanshan? Where can Shanshan be?*

At 2 AM, Jun came home empty-handed. Her face was red, and her hat and scarf had tiny icicles around her mouth. Her eyes showed concern and worry. There were no signs of anger.

For the first time in a long while, Lianlian didn't have Shanshan next to her on the kang.

There was no news for the next two days. Although Jun tried to put on a brave face, Lianlian knew she must be worried sick. They'd heard plenty of horrible stories of young girls being attacked outside their homes.

On the third day, Jun came home from work with a relieved look.

"Aunt Ma called me just before I left work. Shanshan's safe at her home. I'll go pick her up after dinner."

Several hours passed. Jun finally came back. Her face was blue and eyes red.

"Shanshan refused to come back. She'll stay with Aunt Ma for a few days." With that, Jun went to bed.

Aunt Ma was Jun's vocational school classmate. She was the only other person Lianlian knew who was divorced, too. Her violent husband, upon learning of her decision for a divorce, took her younger son away as revenge. That almost killed her. She raised her older son by herself for a few years. Her son was the same age as Lianlian, and the similarity of their situations had made the two families very close. They visited each other often, and the kids played together. Aunt Ma was truly like an aunt to Lianlian and Shanshan, and likewise, Jun was an aunt to her son.

Recently, Aunt Ma got remarried. Her new husband was a man of high social status. Jun had taken the girls to visit the new family just a few weeks before, during the Spring Festival. The new husband had bought tickets for them to go to a huge auditorium to watch the New Year's performance. Aunt Ma had noticed Lianlian was using the wait time and break time to memorize new English words with the little booklet she'd made. Each page had English on one side and Chinese on the other.

"You'll become a professor someday," she proclaimed. A few years earlier, when Lianlian was ten, she had asked, "What do you want to be when you grow up?"

"A professor," Lianlian had replied, though she didn't know what a professor did. She just thought it was someone with the highest possible level of education and the most amount of knowledge, and that society respected it as a career.

"You two should learn from Lianlian," she'd remarked to her son and Shanshan, who were playing hand-clapping games.

Aunt Ma's new house, a 15-minute bike ride from Jun's house, was splendid. Her new husband showed great affection toward her. She looked happy. The boy proudly showed Lianlian and Shanshan his new room, new clothing, and new toys.

When they got home from that visit, Jun had commented, "How showy."

Although Lianlian was happy for Aunt Ma and her son, she had a feeling that they might not see them as often as they had before Aunt Ma remarried.

Aunt Ma came to Jun's house the evening after Jun had tried to fetch Shanshan from her home. She confided in Lianlian, "Your mom fainted last night."

"What?" That shocked Lianlian. She couldn't imagine a powerful person like her mom fainting. But she knew Jun loved Shanshan. It must have been that she loved her too much and never thought she would leave. Jun had mentioned so many times that her girls were her everything, and she'd do anything to keep them.

Aunt Ma confirmed Lianlian's suspicion.

"Your mother told me you two were her entire world. She couldn't imagine a life without Shanshan. As a divorced mother who lost her second son, I understood perfectly. Shanshan broke your mom's heart."

"How is Shanshan?" Lianlian was so eager to know more.

"Shanshan was stubborn and rebellious and refused to bend or apologize. That angered and hurt your mom. She lost control of herself. We would have sent her to the hospital if she hadn't revived. Shanshan is doing fine. She's calm and playing with my son. She just got her first period and needed to change clothes. I gave her my old ones."

Shanshan stayed at Aunt Ma's for a few more days. Lianlian didn't go to see her because she wasn't sure if it would upset her mom.

Then one day, Jun told Lianlian, "Shanshan is going to your father's home. This is a reasonable solution. Shanshan refuses to return home, and I won't allow her back until she admits her mistake and promises not to repeat it."

"What?!" Lianlian was horrified.

Living with Father, who had mistreated us when we were younger? And Shanshan had been so afraid to live with him?

Lianlian had heard grown-ups talking about the rebelliousness of teenagers, especially girls, around the time they got their first period. She wondered if that was what happened to Shanshan. The old saying was that a woman should not drink or touch cold water during her period. She remembered how caring Shanshan was in bringing warm water to her when she got her first period. Too bad Lianlian had not been with Shanshan for her first period. For several nights in a row, Lianlian reached to Shanshan's usual spot next to hers on the kang. She fell into sleep with tears in her eyes and emptiness in her heart.

Shanshan was in the junior division of the same high school. She made it to the same high school the following year. They met at school during recess for two years. Often, it was Shanshan standing by Lianlian's classroom door right after the bell. Then they'd wander on campus until they found a bench or flat place to sit.

"Let me show you the bike! I had to find a nice spot for it this morning." She wanted to drag Lianlian to the parking lot.

"Good for you. Class is about to start," answered Lianlian.

One day, Shanshan showed up with a bright smile. "Look, isn't this shirt nice? I told my friends that Aunt Feng bought it for me."

"Did she?"

"No. Father did. But it sounds better if she did. Plus, they're married, so his money is hers. Father said I can still call her Aunt Feng if I want."

"I guess she can't sew like Mom."

"No, she can't. But we don't need to sew. Father has money to buy from the store."

"I need to return to my class now."

"But we just got here, and we have another 20 minutes."

"I know, but I need to go." Lianlian left with her eyes rolling.

On another day, Shanshan came with a nice bag.

"I brought you goodies!"

"I got some for you, too."

They sat and opened their bags.

"Mom made this steamed bun with red beans, your favorite. To-day's the Moon Festival."

Shanshan looked, and her mouth turned down into a frown. "That's not my favorite anymore. THIS is my favorite." She opened her bag and brought out two mooncakes, each the size of a fist. "One for you, one for me!"

Lianlian didn't move. Moon cakes always brought her terrible memories of her father hoarding them during their only Moon Festival together.

"Are you okay?" asked Shanshan.

"Do you remember the Moon Festival we spent with Father when we were little? When we peeked into Father's inner room to check on his desk? When he held onto all the festival goods and let them go bad without sharing with us?"

"Hmm, yes." Shanshan's voice lowered. "But Father said it was because he was mad at Mom. He said Mom brought the worst out of him."

"And yet, he made his young daughters suffer."

"Mom lost her temper, too."

"But it's different. She may lose her temper, but she would never withhold treatment from her girls to let them suffer. And you said your Aunt Feng was nice. Did she take you to the hospital last week when you had a fever?"

"No. Father did."

"Of course she didn't. But do you remember when your appendix was inflamed three years ago? Mom carried you to the hospital because we didn't have a bike. That was twenty minutes away!"

"Jie. Sorry, I upset you."

"Don't you ever brag about your father and your Aunt Feng in front of me! I am not interested. And take this moon cake away. It makes me sick! Never give me anything bought with his money!"

"Jie. I wanted to share what I have with you. But don't be mad at me. I just couldn't stand Mom anymore. And I had nowhere to go but Father's."

Lianlian sighed. She knew Mom favored her over Shanshan. She also knew too well the desperate feeling of nowhere to go.

The girls continued to meet and spend time together, but Shanshan stopped updating Lianlian on her fancy new life. Yet she couldn't help but tell others who asked and wanted to listen. Everyone wanted to find out everything about Lianlian, and everyone knew Shanshan was her sister.

Lianlian suspected her father had lured Shanshan in the first place, making her pick a fight and then leave home. He was making a statement by letting Shanshan ride a bike and by buying her clothes and goodies from the store. This only added to Lianlian's disregard of her father. She saw Shanshan as a child who was being used as a weapon by her father.

Shanshan wasn't good at filtering what to say or how to say it. She leaked what Bin-Kai and his family thought of Jun and Lianlian. One takeaway was that they thought Jun had brainwashed Lianlian, and as a result, Lianlian was a traitor of the family, too.

No one can brainwash me. I see with my own eyes. I think with my own brain. You have never treated me as family, so I don't consider you my family either!

From that moment on, Lianlian cut off any remaining emotional and physical bond with her father's family, which was already barely any. They became her enemies.

34

Dry-Run College Entrance Exam

After Shanshan left home during Lianlian's first year of high school, Lianlian committed even more effort to studying. She knew Jun poured all the energy and attention outside work to support her, and she didn't want to disappoint her mother.

Jun had hopes that her daughter might carry out her own unfulfilled hopes in life. She had the sense that Lianlian could bring her the glory that she had always wanted to be the most regarded and admired person. Her competitive, recognition-seeking efforts now completely shifted to Lianlian. Her life had a whole new meaning and purpose: to get Lianlian to the highest potential place, whatever that might be.

To Jun's delight, Lianlian seemed to have what it might take to fulfill Jun's dreams. Lianlian was interested in nothing but studying. She was self-directed and didn't need Jun to push her. She had set herself a daily and weekly routine, which she followed with impeccable reliability. Her calm and mellow manner hid a fierce determination, as if she knew where she was going. The only thing that might irritate Lianlian was being told what to do.

Not wanting to distract or pressure Lianlian, Jun constantly thought about ways she could help. Providing enough nutrition topped Jun's daily concerns. Fortunately, these days she could find more desirable goods and produce than in the old days and outside government departments. With more competition, the cost of products had gone down. Jun's salary was enough to supply both of them with ample healthy food.

Ensuring a quiet and non-distracting study environment was another area Jun paid attention to. She asked the neighbor boys many times to lower their voices. Besides making her home noise-free, she also made her office an alternative place for Lianlian to study and accompanied Lianlian there on countless weekends and nights.

Lianlian was ending her first year of high school in July 1979.

"How many final exams are left?" Jun asked casually.

"One for each subject. They all happen in the last three days of the academic year."

"Are you worried about them?"

"Not really. I just do my regular thing."

"No reviews or preparations?"

"I have done them. I keep up with teachers and do my best regularly, and I didn't need to do extra work for finals."

Jun nodded. That reminded her of what she had done. She was a star student in her classes throughout her schooling. Exams never bothered her because she did her regular studies to the best of her ability.

"In that case, how about attending the college entrance exams? They happen right after your school ends." The national college entrance exams took place in high schools' facilities.

"What? The official college entrance exams?" Lianlian was surprised. Those exams had been a north star she had been aiming for, but they still seemed distant.

"Yes. No need for preparation. Just test your ability as it stands right now. Remember, last year, you solved a math problem at the college entrance exam level." Jun referred to the Pythagorean theorem problem when she was tutoring her junior colleagues who'd been preparing for the college entrance exams.

"That was just one math problem, and there must be more hard problems."

"Exactly. You will find out. And you will know how far you are from getting into college."

"The exams are only a few days away."

"Correct. I didn't want you to worry and affect your regular studying. Just do what you can on the exams."

Lianlian thought about it. She disliked being unprepared but was curious about college entrance exams. She wondered about the types of problem and how the test-taking experience would be like .

"Okay, I'll do it. By the way, when did you register me?"

"A few months ago."

It took two-and-a-half days to complete the five subject exams: Math, Physics, Chemistry, Chinese, and Political Science. English was not part of the exams that year.

Of all the test locations, Lianlian's was at her own high school, and the proctor for her exam was Teacher Tuan!

The whole time, Teacher Tuan paced around the room and stopped by Lianlian's desk, looking over her shoulders. That made her very nervous. So much so that she messed up her favorite topic in math, the Pythagorean theorem. This became a source of laughter in their future conversations.

When the exam results came out, Jun was delighted. Lianlian's score was above the cutoff, so she could attend college.

On the registration form, Jun had filled in several medical universities as the desired placements. But the acceptance notice was for a non-ranked technical university in another province. That meant that Lianlian scored below her selected universities and majors and was being placed in a university that didn't have enough enrollment.

Teacher Tuan was extremely concerned. When the acceptance notices came out during the summer school break, he called Jun and Lianlian for a meeting.

"It will be a tremendous waste if Lianlian goes to this technical university this year. This result does not reflect her true ability. Let her stay for one more year in high school."

"It was just a dry run to give her experience," said Jun.

Deep inside, she wanted to send Lianlian to a much better school, and one more year was worth it.

Lianlian didn't want to take the offer. She was not content with her performance and didn't want to go somewhere to study something she hadn't deliberately chosen to study.

The experience familiarized Lianlian with the college entrance exams. She had imagined they'd be very different, but they were just like the exams she took in school. The experience also gave her confidence that she could make it to college, even without preparation.

I want to do more and do better. I know I can! If it takes time to get where I want to go, so be it.

35

COMPETITIONS

The heat of preparing for college entrance exams intensified during the last year of high school. Competitions happened at various levels, not just in spirit, but in practice.

First, within Lianlian's class, students were ranked after each exam on each subject, no matter how small the exam was. The class bulletin board was used exclusively for displaying ranks. Students felt tremendous pressure.

During parent-teacher conferences, students' exams and homework became available for parents to view. This caused tension among the parents. At each conference, several parents would question the exams of top-ranked students, including Lianlian. Her papers were scrutinized by these parents, and some even approached the teachers to argue about her work, as if that would somehow help their own children.

Jun became a target, too. Initially, she reacted defensively. Then she became very cool, letting those absurd adults fight all they wanted. Jun believed in Lianlian and trusted that she was the best in the Ace class, and thus the best in the entire high school.

There was competition at school level, too. Some students from regular classes believed they were as good as students in the Ace classes, and they were sometimes correct. In the school-wide rankings, not all the students in the Ace classes were among those at the very top of the list.

A student named Warina in Class #5 requested to transfer to Ace Class #3 based on two school-wide rankings, where she was among the top 10.

Warina attended junior high in the old town of Hohhot and was very proud that she made it to No. 2 High School. Part of the pride came from her being selected as the Model Youth of the Inner Mongolia region, a political honor that would have been enough to pave her future life if it were during the Cultural Revolution. But that honor was reduced to being a mere honorable mention. Her stay-at-home mother rented a house close to the high school and cooked and cared for her during school. An older relative took care of her father and younger sister, who lived in their home, which was an hour's bike ride from the high school.

Warina brought up the transfer request as if she had the right to do it, a significant move that had never happened before. Teacher Tuan accepted the transfer request after examining her overall performance. Two months later, Warina requested to transfer back to Class #5. Rumor had it that she'd developed a sleeping disorder. That was shocking to many people. Mental health was not a publicly talked-about topic.

Yet Lianlian could see why. During those two months, several simulation tests had happened, each with rankings published. Every day, students were asked to raise their hands if they could answer the teacher's questions. Lianlian saw Warina's hand up less, and her chin got lower.

Teacher Xia, the homeroom teacher for Class #5, said, "It's better to be the best in the regular class than to be at the bottom of the Ace class." She was the chemistry teacher for several classes, including Class #3.

At the city level, several Olympic-style, subject-specific competitions began. High schools sent their best students as representatives, turning the events into contests among schools. Listing the number of medals won soon became standard when a high school introduced itself, and students who triumphed were celebrated as heroes for bringing honor to their school.

The top performers from city-level contests represented their home city at the provincial level.

It didn't surprise Lianlian when she was selected to represent her high school in math, physics, and chemistry. Her best friend Lian #3 had been among those selected in the physics competition, too. However, Lianlian was shocked to learn that she, Lianlian, had been one of the five students chosen to compete in Chinese, and also one of the five selected to compete in English.

Because of the lesser weight Chinese and English had on college entrance exams, compared to math, physics, and chemistry, there were fewer simulation tests and fewer ranks. The selections were partially based on the ranks and partially based on teachers' recommendations.

Lianlian's favorite aspect of studying Chinese as a subject was composition. Teacher Hao, an old gentleman with a pair of thick glasses, had recited her essays several times in class. However, Lianlian was not confident in interpreting ancient Chinese or memorizing poems. But Teacher Hao had recommended her. She tried her best but did not rank in the Chinese competition results.

Students had started learning English in the first year of junior high. All English teachers were Chinese with some English training.

Lianlian's favorite English teacher was the one she had in high school. The school rehired Teacher Gu, who was in her late 50s and already retired, to teach English to the two Ace classes. She was a quiet, small, and kind lady who'd had private teachers at home while growing up. It meant she'd had a rich family before communist China, and her family must have been of a low class during the Cultural Revolution.

Up to that point, the college entrance exam had not included English as a subject. Most students cared little about it. Lianlian cared about English for two reasons. First, it was part of the curriculum, which meant it was valuable for one's education. She would work on it to the best of her ability. Second, Teacher Gu taught it.

Teacher Gu's English pronunciation was pleasant to hear. When she read a passage, the sound flowed smoothly like a breeze of air, with slight ups and downs. Lianlian wondered if her pronunciation was more accurate compared to other English teachers she had had. Teacher Gu's knowledge of English seemed internalized, compared to other English teachers who recited what they'd memorized or referenced dictionaries.

Few students would ask Teacher Gu questions during self-study classes. Teacher Gu had a lot of time to answer Lianlian's questions. She also provided Lianlian with extra materials besides the textbook.

Lianlian realized English was not just about memorization. She saw the language's logic and the patterns of the grammar. Even English words exhibited certain patterns, which made memorizing them a lot easier for her.

Lianlian won a bronze medal in the city-wide English competition and represented her hometown in the provincial competition. Although she did not go very far in that competition, Teacher Gu was extremely proud of her.

"You did well. You will do very well in the future," said Teacher Gu.

"Thank you! Some of the questions I was able to answer based on the extra readings you provided." Lianlian was proud to make Teacher Gu happy.

Placing at the top in math, physics, and chemistry, Lianlian represented her hometown in the provincial competitions. She received city-level gold medals in all three subjects, provincial gold medals for math and physics, and a provincial silver medal for chemistry.

With so many levels of competition and strong pressure from teachers, parents, and peers, there was little talk of people's mental health issues. Warina from Class #5 was the only one Lianlian had heard of.

Students toughed it out.

36

MADAME MARIE CURIE

Life at home was not without conflict.

One day in spring 1979, Lianlian's high school friend invited her to see a movie. It was about a young couple who wanted to get married, but the boy's family disagreed. When Lianlian told Jun about going to see this movie, Jun disapproved, saying it would take Lianlian's time away from studying.

Lianlian wanted to go because several classmates had seen the movie already and had spoken highly of it. She didn't want to be left out. Plus, the movie depicted two people showing affection toward each other, something very new and intriguing to her. It was another area that changes in society had opened up.

"I want to go. I already did all my homework," Lianlian protested.

"How dare you disobey me?" Jun raised her voice.

Ironically, that made Lianlian's desire to go even stronger. She went.

Upon returning, Lianlian entered the yard and could already sense that something serious was about to happen. When she stepped into the room, Jun was holding a wooden stick. Her face was red, and her brow clenched into a hard knot. Without a single word, she swung the stick at Lianlian.

Lianlian twisted her body. The stick landed on her lower back. Anticipating her butt might be the next target, she put her right hand there. Sure enough, the stick hit her hand. She automatically withdrew it because it hurt like hell.

Ouch! She needed her bony hand to write. To protect her hands, she put them in front of her chest and close to her armpits. Yet, it looked as if she was crossing her arms to protest.

Jun was furious. She hasn't been this angry since she was dealing with Shanshan. It made her hit Lianlian harder and with a heavier swing each time.

Lianlian stood there, resolving to let Jun hit her. She didn't beg, and she didn't cry. She didn't know how many times Jun had hit her. With each blow, Jun yelled something like Lianlian being disobedient, disrespectful, and a traitor.

The neighbors heard the commotion. Ge Meng's mother rushed into the house.

"Why, why! What could be the matter that's so terrible it cannot be discussed? Why use physical punishment? She's a high schooler," she protested, taking the stick out of Jun's hand.

Jun took a heavy breath. "She didn't listen to me." Letting out a long exhale, Jun spoke slowly, "She disobeyed me. She tried to upset me."

Ge Meng's mother turned to Lianlian and reprimanded her. "Why didn't you listen to your mom? It isn't easy for her to raise you alone. You shouldn't upset her."

Lianlian did not answer. She didn't feel a need to answer. There was no justice for children, no matter what. She would always be the one to blame in this and any other situation—*I had openly disobeyed her; therefore, I deserved to be punished.*

There were several other reasons Jun had become so upset: The movie's plot reminded Jun of her marriage; it was the first time Lianlian had openly disobeyed her, and she wanted to show she was in control; and most importantly, this had happened soon after Shanshan left, and Jun felt insecure that Lianlian would leave her, too.

Jun had occasionally used corporal punishment while Lianlian and Shanshan were young children, a common practice for all parents. But it had not happened for years. This would be the last time she hit Lianlian, who had just turned sixteen.

It was not the last time TV or movies became a topic of discussion between Jun and Lianlian, though.

"There's a TV series about the life of Madame Marie Curie that'll air each Sunday, starting this week," Jun announced one day in the fall of 1979.

In school, students had learned about several scientists in physics and chemistry, and the prestige of the Nobel Prize. Lianlian reported to Jun whatever happened at school, so Jun knew Lianlian admired Madame Curie.

"Wow! But I have to study. We have bonus math classes on Sunday mornings. I also have extra physics and chemistry homework to do."

"This TV program is in the evening. Just finish all you must do and save the evening for it."

"My friend and I are doing several topics together after the bonus class. I count on doing the extra homework in the evenings."

For a long time, Lianlian and her classmate Lian #3 had spent Sundays studying together in Jun's office.

"Bring her along. Does she like Madame Curie?"

"Yes. We all do. As far as I know, all girls admire her."

"Then definitely bring her along."

Lianlian contemplated. "How long is each episode? How many episodes?"

"Four episodes, about two hours each. Treat it as a break from studying."

Two hours! A total of eight hours! That is a long break! I could do so much in eight hours.

Jun saw what was going on in Lianlian's mind.

"You know how you have 10-minute breaks between classes at school? That's for allowing your brain to take a break so that it can function better and be more productive. In the same way, watching this TV program will only do you good, so you can be more productive. Just plan accordingly so that you don't miss any homework."

That made sense to Lianlian.

"Okay. I'll ask Lian #3 if she wants to join me for the TV show. I'll try to finish everything during the day."

"Lunch will be ready when you two are home."

Lian #3 would join Lianlian at her home after math class and loved the lunches Jun prepared. After that, the two girls would skip the nap and go to Jun's office to spend the afternoon studying together.

When Lianlian told Lian #3 about the TV program, she said her mom would take her to a friend's house to watch, because it would be too late for her to bike home after the program.

For four Sundays, Jun biked with Lianlian to her office building, which had a large color TV in the room next to her office. There was a large group of other people watching, too. They all knew Lianlian was in the Ace class and must be an excellent student. Some of them said to her, "Study hard and you might turn out just like Madame Curie."

That statement might be an obvious message to many grown-ups. To Lianlian, though, there were different takeaways from the show. It was tragic that Mr. Curie died because he was absent-minded and was crushed by a horse cart. What impressed Lianlian the most was that Madame Curie continued their joint scientific explorations alone after her husband died—and that she succeeded.

That Madame Curie was just as competent as her husband amazed Lianlian. It was as if they'd shared each other's brains. It didn't start that way, but it ended that way. They were drawn to each other because of their shared ability to converse at a high level about complex matters. Working side by side intellectually was more inspiring to Lianlian than winning the Nobel Prize twice, which was admirable, too. That might have been when the seed was planted in her mind to seek a life partner who would be her equal.

37

College Application

Time passed quickly. Before long, it was the last semester of high school.

At one parent-teacher-student conference, the focus was on preparing college application forms. The students had to declare which universities they wished to apply to and what majors they wanted to study.

After covering the general procedure for college applications, each student and his or her parents had a group meeting with multiple teachers.

"Lianlian should go to one of the top two universities. It would be a waste of talent if she went anywhere else," Teacher Tuan said firmly.

The top two universities were Peking University and Tsinghua University. Founded in 1898, Peking University (PKU) was often referred to as China's Harvard. Tsinghua University was founded in 1891 and called China's Massachusetts Institute of Technology (MIT).

Teacher Tuan continued, "I should also mention another option, the newer but very promising University of Science and Technology of China (USTC). The government has invested a lot of funding and resources in USTC. Some of the more cutting-edge majors may offer more opportunities there."

The Chinese Academy of Sciences founded USTC in 1958, intending to produce a high-level workforce within the spheres of economics, defense, science, and technology. It was in the top 16 national key universities in 1959, and a tier 2 national key university in the recent new classification. In 1980, it was in the very top tier in the college admissions process.

"Lianlian should attend Peking University to study physics," Teacher Lu chipped in. He was the physics teacher for the two Ace classes and four other classes. Quiet and reserved, he was thoughtful when he spoke, even while teaching.

"Oh? Why?" Jun asked. She'd heard Lianlian saying a lot about math at home, but not as much about physics.

"She's the gold medal recipient for the regional Olympics in physics. That shows how good she is. Because of Lee Tsung-Dao and Yang Chen-Ning, physics is the hottest major now in China. And of course, if you're going to study physics at a top university, it has to be Peking University," explained Teacher Lu.

Lee Tsung-Dao and Yang Chen-Ning were both Chinese American physicists. In 1957, they won the Nobel Prize in physics together. They were the first Chinese winners and among the youngest winners ever, 31 and 34.

"But Lianlian was the gold medalist for the math Olympics, too. And she won the silver medal for chemistry," said Teacher Tuan.

"I think Lianlian should go to Beijing Normal University, which produces future teachers. She has shown excellence in all her courses, including English and Chinese. She's not like most students who are good at logical subjects but bad at literature and language, or vice versa," said Teacher Xia, who taught chemistry.

All three of them looked at Lianlian with big smiles.

Like a fly on the wall, Lianlian had been listening and amused by her teachers' making claims on her behalf. She had not had a chance to express her views. When they all looked at her, she became self-conscious and blushed.

But before she spoke, Jun said, "It seems we've narrowed it down to four top universities: Tsinghua, Peking, USTC, and Beijing Normal University." She looked at the marks on the draft application form.

"The top universities will be among the first round of admission processing. Missing one of them will not send her file to another one. We need to focus on just one. Beijing Normal University is in a lower tier." Teacher Lu was thoughtful as he reminded everyone of the ins and outs of the college admission process.

Peking, Tsinghua, and USTC were the only top-tier universities that received priority access to all the college-eligible applications during the first round. The unselected applicants would go to the next tier. The workflow continued until all universities felt satisfied or all files had been processed. Accordingly, an applicant should strategically list their preferred universities, ensuring that their first and second choices are from different tiers. If the first choice rejected the application, the system would automatically forward it to the universities in the next tier.

All three teachers and Jun looked at each other, then turned to Lianlian.

The first sentence she said during the conference came out without hesitation.

"Not Tsinghua University!"

That shocked everyone. They froze. The three teachers' faces changed from alarmed to puzzled.

Jun was the first to speak after that.

"Her father graduated from it."

The teachers looked at each other, then at Jun and Lianlian.

Teacher Xia asked, "Why does it matter?"

"Exactly. You can still attend it," said Teacher Tuan.

Teacher Lu didn't speak but had a thoughtful look on his face.

Lianlian exclaimed, "No—I never want people to say, 'The daughter followed in her father's footsteps.' I want to hear 'The daughter is better than the father.'"

She was surprised at her own voice. But it was something she had been thinking about for a long time. She wanted her future to have nothing to do with her father. Absolutely nothing. That included not sharing the same alma mater.

She could feel her face flushing. She looked at the three teachers and Jun with a serious expression, making sure they'd understood what she said.

Teacher Lu had an appreciative look on his face. Teacher Xia grinned from ear to ear.

"Very good! Very good!" Teacher Tuan looked at Lianlian with an air of approval. Of the three teachers, he knew the most about her family dynamics. He sensed Lianlian's father was a factor behind Lianlian's unwavering focus on studying.

"Then we should put Peking University. It's the most prestigious, historically and now," said Teacher Lu with satisfaction.

"What about the majors?" Jun asked.

All three teachers looked at Lianlian and asked simultaneously, "What do you enjoy most?"

Lianlian felt calmer now, but she was uncertain about the majors. "I like all subjects."

"That doesn't help. We need to narrow it down to the majors that offer the most potential for your future," Teacher Tuan pointed out.

"I still think physics is the one. The work of Lee and Yang has made it a highly desirable major, and I can only imagine that more opportunities will arise," Teacher Lu noted.

"True. But then, mathematician Chen Jingrui has also raised the level of interest in math in the country. The recognition of his contribution can be seen in the government's encouragement of more young people to devote themselves to basic math research," Teacher Tuan pointed out.

Chen Jingrui's story came out in 1978 and became a national sensation. As a mathematician, he'd spent half his life researching and solving a theoretical question. The most amazing part of the story was his determination, even while living a stressful, frugal life. The Red Guards targeted him physically and emotionally. He had been labeled a Stinking Old Ninth, a term for intellectuals who didn't follow the Communist Party during the Cultural Revolution. He lived in a tiny room for years with little money to buy food, and had several health problems, some of which led to hospitalization and surgeries. Yet he continued his research and was regarded by the global mathematical community as the inventor of Chen's Theorem and Chen Prime.

Teacher Xia laughed. "I will not join in on this friendly competition and insist on her studying chemistry. Again, I truly believe Lianlian will excel at anything she wants to study. Should we identify a major that could be most influential for the future, rather than the past?"

"Or a major that combines multiple basic subjects?" Teacher Lu added.

"What about computer science? I read about it in the newspaper yesterday. It's a fresh field and has a lot of potential," Teacher Tuan suggested, with his fingers pointing at the major on the list in the application form.

"I agree. I read about it too in a magazine. It's fascinating," Teacher Lu nodded.

"From what I've read," Teacher Tuan said, "computer science builds on both math and physics. That would be ideal for Lianlian."

"This reminds me that my neighbor's son was admitted by Hua Zhong College of Technology. He was in a computer-related major. He said he'd wear a white coat and be disinfected before entering the lab," Jun recalled. She was referring to Ge Meng's big brother, Ge Ang, two years ahead of Lianlian and a cohort of 1978. Lianlian learned later that Ang's major was microelectronics, a branch of computer science.

Teacher Xia asked Lianlian, "What do you think? Do you like computer science?"

Lianlian did not know what a computer was or what computer science was about. But she trusted her teachers and liked their reasoning.

"If it combines subjects I enjoy, I should do well," said Lianlian.

"Sure, you will, no matter what you do. But what's important is that you like it." Teacher Xia grinned and patted Lianlian's back. She openly showed her excitement and happiness for Lianlian. Direct and affectionate, she had no problem showing favoritism towards Lianlian in class, making classmates envious.

"Great! Computer science it is!" Teacher Lu exclaimed, unlike his usual reserved self.

"What about the non-key universities?" Jun pointed to the application form.

"She won't go to any of them. You can put down whatever you want." Teacher Tuan smiled.

Jun put down some medical colleges in Hohhot.

"It's always helpful to have a doctor in the house," she remarked. That was a common notion among all parents.

Computer science at Peking University became Lianlian's first choice. She did not realize just how visionary her teachers were.

38

END OF HIGH SCHOOL

The three-day-long college entrance exams happened July 7–9, 1980. Students from across the entire country took the same tests on the same days. Six subjects were covered, and each took three hours. For science students, the total scores included 100% of math, physics, chemistry, Chinese literature and political science, but only 30% of English. Math had bonus questions worth 10% of the points.

Lianlian's high school hosted her exam. This time, to her relief, Teacher Tuan was not her proctor. She handled the tests with quiet confidence. It was helpful to be at a familiar location, facing familiar question types and test formats. She answered every question on the test, including the bonus ones in math.

Jun prepared nutritious meals and eliminated any distractions. She picked up Lianlian with her bike when Lianlian finished morning exams and dropped Lianlian back off for the afternoon exams. Lianlian saved commute time and took a nap during the break. She was lucky. Not every student could take the exams at a familiar location or had the option of taking a break during the day.

After years of preparation, the highly anticipated college entrance exams were over in the blink of an eye.

High school graduation occurred the following week. There were no gowns, caps, or hoods, and no families brought yummy food or flowers. Students sat together in the auditorium to go through the motions. With the college entrance exam results and college placements still unknown, anxiety was widespread, and the graduation program held little appeal.

The school's Communist Party Head, a woman in her mid-40s, led the program. Her face was shining, and her eyes were sparkling. She proved to be the most excited person in the whole auditorium. She appeared to have won a top prize.

Well, the school did. The leader announced the high school had been ranked No. 1 in the region based on the total number of medals received in the Provincial Olympic Competitions. She wanted to give awards to a handful of students who'd brought pride to the school and asked the winners to come to the stage when she announced their names.

In anticipation of being called, Lianlian stood and prepared to walk toward the stage. But her name never came. The woman put her notepad away and was about to give out the awards to those who lined up on the podium.

Lianlian didn't know what to do.

Did I hear her wrong? But those standing there were the winners. Should I sit, or should I just walk up to the front?

Teacher Tuan waved his hand as if to stop the woman. He walked toward Lianlian and reached for her hand. He led Lianlian to the center of the stage. It was a long walk for Lianlian. Everyone watched her. It made her uncomfortable.

Teacher Tuan nodded at the woman, and said, "You missed the very top student who earned the most medals for the school."

The woman looked at Lianlian and shot a glance toward Lianlian's feet. That reminded Lianlian that she'd done this in the past on various occasions when someone introduced Lianlian to her. There was no mistake she disliked Lianlian, although Lianlian couldn't think of what she had done to offend this woman. Few people in high school knew of Bin-Kai's reputation. Since Jun was divorced, something which was still taboo, Lianlian could only imagine that the woman's dislike of her had to do with that.

Lianlian reminded herself: *There will always be people who dislike you and who snub you regardless of what you do.*

The winners didn't receive any trophies or plaques. Instead, the awards were practical things. Lianlian received three reference books: an encyclopedia of Chinese history, an English-Chinese dictionary for Science and Technology terminology, and a large English dictionary. In addition, she received high-quality pens and several fancy notebooks. These items accompanied her for years in her future studies. Much later, whenever she struggled or doubted herself, the reference books reminded her of her hard work and achievements.

39

College Admission

The college entrance exam results came out. The school put up big character posters around the bulletin boards and on the walls of the buildings. There was no privacy, every student's total score was on display. Lianlian topped the list, with a total score of 456. She placed No. 1 in the capital city of Hohhot and No. 2 in the Inner Mongolia Autonomous Region. A student from Baotou, another major city in Inner Mongolia, had a score a few points higher than hers.

Colleges would announce the first round of decisions at the start of August, with the remaining decisions in mid-August. Lianlian should be the first to receive an acceptance announcement in the beginning of August.

Or so she and everyone else thought.

One week after the college entrance exam results came out, Jun received a call from the provincial college admissions office: "Please come with your daughter."

A gentleman greeted them. "Good afternoon. This is Professor Zhao from The University of Science and Technology of China, USTC."

Professor Zhao sat on one side of a conference table. Middle-aged, average-built, and clean-shaven with a wide forehead, he stood up and walked around the table to shake their hands.

"Very nice to meet you. Please, sit." He had a big smile on his face.

It flattered Lianlian that a university professor had shaken hands with her as if she were a grown-up or someone important.

"Your daughter did well in the college entrance exams, and you should be very proud of her," he said to Jun, then nodded at Lianlian.

"I am proud," Jun smiled.

Professor Zhao turned to Lianlian and asked, "What is your first choice of university?"

"Peking University, computer science," Lianlian answered quietly.

There was something on his face that seemed very welcoming and encouraging. Lianlian didn't feel bad that she hadn't chosen USTC.

"I see. A great university and a great major." He sipped the tea.

"The reason I'm hoping to talk with you two is that we're building a special program at USTC for the first time, and we want to enroll you, Zhou Lianlian."

Jun and Lianlian looked at each other, then looked back at him.

Jun said, "We did not apply to USTC."

"It's not a problem. The question is, will Lianlian be interested in this new program? If so, we can bypass Peking University."

"Oh?" Jun's eyes opened wide.

"Oh?" Lianlian's mouth made an O shape.

"Chinese government funds USTC and wants it to represent China's advancement in all science and technology disciplines." Professor Zhao drank more tea.

"To learn from developed countries in those subjects where China is behind, we're sending our youngest and brightest students to study abroad. This will be the first year we do so." He paused to note their reactions. Lianlian's heart jumped fast. She wished he could speed up his speech. Jun's eyes sparkled.

"For the selected students, we will offer scholarships during the entire period of their study. We start by paying their travel expenses to the university. Then they'll be grouped into majors and countries to study. They'll have intensive language training before going to the designated countries."

"How many students do you select?" Jun asked.

"In Inner Mongolia, we select six, the top six. Lianlian is one of them." Professor Zhao sipped the tea again. The fact he was drinking tea instead of smoking impressed Lianlian.

Jun and Lianlian looked at each other again. Lianlian saw the excitement in her mother's eyes.

"Do you know what major I might study?" Lianlian immediately considered her question unwise. They may not have gotten that far yet.

"Yes. You will be in the biochemistry major and travel to Germany after language training on the USTC campus. I saw your chemistry score in the college entrance exams."

"Wow, what?" Lianlian doubted her hearing.

"I know you learned English, not German. But I have confidence that you will grasp an adequate enough level of German quickly. You are a fast learner, aren't you?" Professor Zhao's face held a gentle smile.

"I know nothing of the German language. How long do I need to study it before going abroad?"

Lianlian imagined she was on the USTC campus, frantically memorizing unfamiliar words and grammar—German must have those, too, just like English.

"That depends on how fast you learn. I expect up to one year. You might go in eight months."

"What happens after she finishes school overseas?" Jun asked.

"We hope she can go as far as she wants, all the way to the highest degree. Then she would come back to hold a prestigious position as a scientist."

"Or a professor?" Lianlian interrupted suddenly, then covered her mouth with her hand. She'd only contemplated becoming a professor. The idea of being a scientist was new.

"That is possible. We don't know that far yet, but we know people like you will become national treasures, and you will make significant contributions to China's science and technology development."

Lianlian constantly checked Jun's face to make sure she hadn't misheard. She hadn't.

"Do we need to decide soon?" asked Jun.

"Yes, I need to hear from you by tomorrow at the latest. We need to make sure we have six students. If Lianlian is not interested, I need to move down the rank to approach another student. But I hope you are interested. It is a grand future for you. I can't imagine a better opportunity."

Professor Zhao said it as if he were a family member, with frankness and no deception. He seemed to mean what he said. That was refreshing. A lot of times, people spoke with a hidden meaning or coded language, forcing their listeners to decipher their true intentions.

"We can get back to you by then," said Jun with certainty.

"Just call me at this number any time during business hours. I will be here for the next few days. You can ask me questions you may think of." Professor Zhao passed Jun a business card after writing a phone number on it.

Jun and Lianlian left the office. On the back of the bike, Lianlian couldn't stop saying, "Wow! Wow!" Jun said nothing, but she smiled the brightest smile. Her mind ran fast. What an honor. What a payoff for all the hard work and high expectations!

Instead of going home, Jun biked to the high school. Excited, she knocked on Teacher Tuan's office. Surprised, he ushered them into the office. Jun debriefed him. Without hesitation, Teacher Tuan said, "Lianlian should go to USTC."

Teacher Xia's office was two doors away. She heard Jun and Lianlian and was right there in front of them. Wiping her tears, she was non-stop talking, "This result is so much better, so much better! They singled you out, just as it should be."

To Lianlian, that was the most meaningful aspect of the entire matter—she'd been chosen in a specific and important way. It was truly an honor.

Plus, up to this moment, she had never heard of anyone going abroad to study, let alone dreamed such a thing would happen to her.

Teacher Lu was not in his office. Jun and Lianlian knew he would concur. At this point, there was not much to discuss.

From the phone in Teacher Tuan's office, Jun called Professor Zhao. Lianlian put her head next to the receiver.

"You and Lianlian made the right decision. Expect to receive the admission letter in the mail soon," he said with confidence.

USTC is in Hefei, Anhui province, far from Hohhot. A southern city, it had humid summers and chilly winters. There were no air conditioners during the summer. The government had a policy of not allowing cities south of the Yangtze River to have any heaters in the winter.

Jun and Lianlian struggled to find a bamboo blanket or bamboo pillow cover, essential for getting through the hot summer nights because they helped lower the body's temperature.

Jun made a heavy comforter with extra layers of cotton for the harsh winter.

Several of her female friends donated their used shoes and clothes.

July went. August came. Lianlian became uneasy because she should have received the admission letter by now.

"Maybe they lost the mail?" She wondered for days.

Jun called the regional college admissions office and was told the entire process was delayed.

August 7th came.

"Mail for you! Congratulations!" The mailman gave Lianlian a thin letter and grinned at her.

Lianlian grabbed the letter hungrily. But at first glance at the front cover, she froze. She saw Peking University written on the envelope.

Is this a mistake?

Flipping the letter a few times, she felt her disbelief increase. Reluctantly, she opened it. It was the official admission letter, welcoming her to the computer science department at Peking University.

What happened to USTC?! To biochemistry?! To studying abroad in Germany?!

Jun went to the regional college admissions office and talked with the gentleman who had arranged the meeting between them and Professor Zhao.

Peking University and Tsinghua University found out they had not had first access to the six top applicants that USTC had secretly removed. They became furious and threatened to withdraw all future recruiting efforts from the region. The regional college admission office yielded, and USTC returned the six files. That caused a slight delay in the entire process, and at last Lianlian received her admission letter from PKU.

Jun had had conflicting feelings after agreeing to let Lianlian attend USTC. Although exciting and glamorous, she was uncertain what might happen to Lianlian when she was far away in a foreign country. She had hidden her feelings during the college preparation time. *It is too late to change the plan. I hope things will work out. Lao Tian Ye (God), help Lianlian!* She had sent prayers often.

When Lianlian presented the admission letter from PKU, she was surprised to see her mom's relieved face.

"It's closer to home. Just an overnight train ride. It has a familiar climate. And it's THE top university."

For two days, Lianlian thought about the USTC offer and its disappearance.

Things can be so unpredictable. First was the offer. Who would have expected it? None of my teachers had heard of it, nor could they find a better opportunity than this. And then, it disappears beyond anyone's control, and before anything could actually happen. To be fair, PKU is your first choice. You lost nothing. And you should grab this opportunity in case it disappears, too.

But the studying abroad idea had become a seed planted in her mind.

College admissions were one hot topic those days. "So-and-so's kids got admission letters from such-and-such universities" was a common refrain among grownups. They chatted while waiting in line at the store, at gatherings, and anywhere else.

By the time the entire college admission process finished, the newspaper announced the national acceptance rate to be 8.41%. For comparison, the acceptance rate had been 5.98% in 1979, 6.59% in 1978, and 4.74% in 1977. In Inner Mongolia, the acceptance rate was 4%.

Most of Lianlian's classmates performed as expected, even though many of them were nervous and doubtful. For them, selecting universities and majors ahead of the entrance exams was beneficial.

Unsurprisingly, Cat King was admitted to Tsinghua University, and Lian #3 would major in physics at Beijing Industry University.

But one star student became a surprise.

Lianlian's best friend, Lian #2, didn't do well. She knew it right after taking the tests but couldn't do much about it. Her top choice had been Beijing Normal University. That didn't happen. By the time her file passed down through the tiers, most of her other choices had finished their admissions. She eventually got admitted to her last choice, Inner Mongolia Normal University. In her case, applying to universities and majors after the exams might have helped.

Another accomplished student made the mistake of putting a third-tier university as his second choice. He attended that university despite his high scores.

What was truly remarkable was that every single member of the Ace Class #3 made it to college. It was the first time that any high school class in the region had had 100% college admission. Years later, during several reunions and personal visits, Lianlian's high school teachers and classmates reminisced about their entire class's achievement. They learned no other class had ever sent all members to college. The pride of having been part of the Ace Class #3 would stay with Lianlian, her classmates, and her teachers.

The neighbor boy Ge Meng planned to study at Inner Mongolia University. It pleased his mother that he'd stay local. Warina from Class #5 was admitted to the Mongol Special Class at PKU. The Inner Mongolia Region collaborated with PKU to form a special class of Mongolian students who promised to come back home after graduating. Lianlian was thrilled that a classmate from high school would attend the same university.

Lianlian heard that Hei Guo Di didn't make it to college. Her score was sufficient for admission to the civil engineering vocational school, and she hoped to follow in her parents' footsteps and work at their institute.

College entrance results became a huge PR matter a few years after Lianlian graduated high school. Newspapers and local TV channels would report on them, and special interviews would be conducted. But in her year, 1980, that didn't happen. Besides the overall summary of the college entrance exam results, no individual schools or students were named.

No one could tell what might have happened if Lianlian had gone to USTC, then Germany, to study biochemistry, but the USTC experience was the spark that led to Lianlian's sky-high dream of studying abroad. Lianlian felt fortunate to be at the right place at the right time for a great opportunity to get a high-quality education based on ability and choice. She had no regrets and only gratitude that she ultimately would enter PKU. She promised herself that she would value this life-saving opportunity to the best of her ability.

At that point in her life, Lianlian couldn't have known that studying computer science at PKU would lead to such fascinating innovations. She would witness China's great leap forward under Deng Xiaoping and Zhao Ziyang.

Many months later, after she'd started college, she developed a deeper understanding of Teacher Lu's suggestion that she should study at Peking University. In a congratulatory letter to Lianlian, he reminded her to appreciate her opportunity, saying it had been his dream back in 1961.

"...I always wanted to study physics at Peking University, and I was thrilled when I was the top applicant in the entire region. But the landlord class of my family crushed my dream. My only choice was to attend Inner Mongolia Normal University to become a teacher for high schools because they were in high demand."

Lianlian treasured his letter and his words because they contributed to a new perspective she was forming: *I should treasure what life offers and never take it for granted.*

40

ROAD AHEAD

At seventeen, standing on the train station platform of her hometown—Hohhot, the Blue City—Lianlian was bidding farewell to Jun, Shanshan, her high school teachers, and several classmates. She was to take an overnight train to Beijing by herself.

"Look who else is going to Beijing on the same train today!" Teacher Tuan gestured to a tall figure surrounded by a group of people on the other side of the same car.

Lianlian's heart jumped fast, and she blushed at the sight of her "Cat King." As if hearing what Teacher Tuan said, Cat King looked her way and walked quickly toward her group.

"Hi, Teacher Tuan, Teacher Xia, and Teacher Lu, I was hoping to see you all here." He shook hands with each of them. As his parents greeted the teachers, he stood in front of Lianlian, his eyes sparkling.

"Hi. I thought you might leave today."

"Oh. Hi. Hmm. How did you know?" Lianlian tried to calm down her heartbeat.

"When I visited Teacher Tuan to say goodbye, he mentioned it. My father was lucky to get two tickets for today's train." There was that carefree style, easy-going manner, and the confidence in his voice and his whole being that Lianlian had always liked.

"Two tickets?"

"My father is coming to help me get settled. We'll stay at a relative's for three days before school starts."

"Good for you." Lianlian wished her mother could go with her.

"Where are you and your mother staying in Beijing?" Cat King asked.

"I am going by myself. We, hmm… There is no where for my mom to stay." There was no need to mention financial constraints.

A surprise turned into admiration on Cat King's face. "Do you, will you need some help to settle on campus? My father and I can be there. PKU is only one street away from Tsinghua."

"Thank you. I think I can handle it." Lianlian said, even though she was not very sure. She was not used to accepting other people's help.

Indeed, we'll be just one street away from each other. But does he like me more than just a classmate? She asked herself silently.

Lianlian looked around. No trace of her father. *Of course, he wouldn't be here.* Lianlian shook her head as if to brush away the negative thoughts.

When the college entry exam results came out, it had surprised and thrilled Bin-Kai that his daughter ranked No. 1 in the city and No. 2 in the region. He had expressed paternal pride, declaring, "Like father, like daughter."

"Will she attend Tsinghua University as you did?" asked a co-worker.

Silence encompassed Bin-Kai. He didn't know. He realized how little he knew his firstborn.

When was the last time I saw her? Two years ago? How tall is she now?

Guilt hit him.

I should have been more present in her life. I should treat her as my child, not as a pawn for her mom.

He told Shanshan, "Ask your sister if she needs any help to prepare for college. It must cost a lot. I can offer money."

Shanshan reported back a few days later. "Lianlian said she needs nothing from you, not your money, not your care, nothing. She said you should stop telling people you have anything to do with her college exam result or her upbringing."

Bin-Kai's heart turned icy.

She was right. Look what you did. You deserve her disdain.

He stopped talking about Lianlian or responding to anyone who brought up her name. When Lianlian didn't visit him before heading to college, it confirmed his fear: she was cutting him out of her life.

As if things couldn't get worse, his father, Mr. Zhou, lost his temper with him and chewed him out.

"Why such cruelty towards your own blood? Your ma would slap your face if she were still alive. Don't you forget, Lianlian is our first grandchild."

"Ba, I hear you. I'll do better in the future."

Ma, rest in peace. Your blood is still your blood, and I will make up for what I did to Lianlian. He sent a silent message to his mother.

Shanshan helped with Lianlian's preparation for departure. She had been going on about her sister to anyone who would listen. She had been proud of Lianlian her whole young life, but this moment was the pinnacle.

One day, it dawned on Shanshan that her big sister would no longer be at school. That realization crushed her. Many times in the past two years, Shanshan had asked Lianlian to help her with homework. They would sit together on a bench during afternoon recess. Shanshan treasured those moments with Lianlian—for her, they had been about much more than just the homework. Shanshan couldn't imagine school without Lianlian.

"You have only one more year of high school. Work hard so you can get into a college in Beijing, and we'll be together again," Lianlian assured Shanshan.

"But I've never been away from you for long."

"I'll be back home for the spring festival and summer break. By summer, your college decision should be final."

And I'll always be there for you and protect you! Privately, Lianlian recited her childhood promise to herself.

Lianlian felt pride and joy upon receiving blessings from Jun's siblings, her aunt Xia, and uncles Xi-Chang and Xi-Dan. As in the past, Xia sent a big box of her own used clothes. But this time, she included several pieces of new clothing. Xi-Chang and Xi-Dan sent money to buy things for college.

Xi-Chang promised, "I'll visit you on campus!"

Xi-Dan wrote in a letter, "I never thought a member of our family would bring so much honor—attending the best university!"

Going to college meant leaving her hometown and saying good-bye to family, teachers, and classmates. Moved by the same sense of farewell and desire to remember, a group of close classmates and Lianlian gathered to take pictures of various landmarks in the city. One girl borrowed a camera from her father. It produced square, black-and-white, 2" x 2" pictures and required technical skills to use—which apparently, they didn't have. Blurriness and misalignment marked many images, and in some, the subjects were too far away and looked tiny.

To Lianlian's relief, a few photos taken at the museum were worth keeping. Lianlian had really wanted to capture the museum on film. The white horse, galloping into the blue sky under the bright sunshine was an image that Lianlian wanted to remember. Even though she knew it might not be perfect, or look different up close, she still loved it just as it was. From street level, the horse appeared even more majestic and spectacular.

Most importantly, the horse held a deeper meaning for her. The statue was facing Beijing, a city that held personal significance for her now that she was heading there for college. The horse jumped forward fearlessly under the boundless sky, and Lianlian found that same courageous spirit in herself: *only the sky should be my limit.*

A week before Lianlian's departure to Beijing, Jun came home from work and said, "I told my co-workers you're leaving in ten days, and they send their best wishes. Maling's mom said that if you want, you can go to Beijing three days earlier and stay with Maling."

"I don't remember Maling. Have I ever met her?"

"Maling left home to work in Beijing right after middle school. She's five years older than you. You met her when she was still in school, a long time ago."

"Is she nice?"

"We last saw her when she was thirteen; she was pleasant then. As the old saying goes, a three-year-old shows her nature; a seven-year-old her future temperament. She should still be a nice person."

"It must be nice to work in Beijing."

"It should be better than working in Hohhot. She's a lucky girl."

"What would I do with my wooden chest?" asked Lianlian.

Every household had wooden chests for storing items. Spacious, they required at least two people to carry them. Many featured a hinged lid and a handle on either side for lifting.

Based on pictures in the housing brochures for both PKU and USTC, Jun had designed this wooden chest and hired a carpenter to make it. The smaller size, aided by a removable lid, permitted placement in crowded areas. It required two people to carry, even when empty. They painted the inside shiny yellow, and the outside smooth maroon. Jun and Lianlian had shopped for a new lock for it.

"Ask Maling to store it temporarily for you. Prepare a separate bag for your short-term needs for those three days. You can check if you need to buy more items in Beijing before school starts."

Lianlian had left her mom before, yet this departure remained unsettling. She was often mistaken for being in her early twenties when she was only seventeen. It wasn't solely her looks. Her mother's friends said she talked and presented herself as if she were much older. Despite her age and appearance, she still depended on her mother for key decisions.

Lianlian thought of her mom's childhood. After having lost her own parents, she'd became guardian for herself and her younger sister Xia. Lianlian reminded herself: *if Mom survived without her parents, I can, too. Besides, I'll be by myself once I'm in college. What difference does it make if I go three days earlier? It'll give me time to learn about Beijing.*

"Sure. I'll go early."

"Leaving early means you'll avoid the crowds, too. Most universities in Beijing open on the same day. The train will be busy."

Despite the fact she was purchasing an off-peak ticket, Jun still needed to reach out to her friends' friends to get it via the "back-door."

Lianlian's excitement soon overcame her anxiety.

I'll be on the train by myself... going to Beijing! To the best university in China! I cannot wait to start my life at PKU!

READING GROUP DISCUSSION QUESTIONS

(More can be found at AppleAnBooks.com)

General Questions

1. What did you like best about ***Daughter of Blue City***, and what did you like least? Why?

2. Do you feel a connection with a particular character? If so, who, and why?

3. Which aspects of the book can you personally relate to?

Questions on Content

1. What have you learned from the book about China's history and politics? Is it consistent with, or different from, what you had understood about China before you read the book?

2. The story covers many events that took place between 1966 and 1980 that helped shape Lianlian's life. Some occurred at national and regional levels, and some took place locally or within the family. Which moments do you think most

influenced the development of Lianlian's character and temperament? Which moment or event do you think was the most important turning point in Lianlian's life? Why?

3. Which characters played an important role, either positive or negative, in Lianlian's life at different stages?

4. How do you feel about the relationship between Lianlian and Jun? Between Lianlian and Shanshan? Between Lianlian and Bin-Kai?

5. At what moment did Lianlian's survival instinct kick in and change her behavior?

6. What do you think the two sisters' respective future lives might be like? How might Lianlian evolve or change after entering PKU? Would Shanshan make it to attend college in Beijing?

7. Does the story have universal significance? Does it remind you of your childhood or the childhoods of people you know?

8. The story explores several overarching themes and important lessons Lianlian learned. What themes and lessons can you identify?

Questions on Writing

1. What makes this book engaging? Are there sections that really drew you in and made the story come alive for you?

2. Are there any parts of the book where you felt lost or needed more information? Was this because of the writing, or because of your unfamiliarity with what was happening in China during that period?

3. Is the mostly-chronological structure of the book effective at depicting the ever-changing environments, Lianlian's observations and reflections, and the overall story?

4. This historical novel is based on actual events. The main characters are fictionalized, but they, too, are based on real people. Do you think the stories and characters, along with their thoughts, actions, and emotions, are realistic? If so, what has the author done to achieve that realism? If not, how could the author have helped bring them more to life?

5. Are the socio-political events effectively blended into the narrative to provide contexts and settings? How well does the author portray the impacts of these events?

6. What do you think were the author's goals when she wrote this book?

7. If you could chat with the author, what would you ask?

Dear Reader

If you enjoyed this book, please leave a review to help other readers decide if this is a book they will enjoy.

If you would like to read more of Apple's literary journey, including news, updates, freebies, media coverages, etc., please sign up for her free newsletters at https://appleanbooks.substack.com/ or with the following QR code.

Apple An's Book Bytes
(AABB) Newsletters

Thank you!

From the multi-award-winning author

Apple An

Visit AppleAnBooks.com

Voices Heard Publishing, LLC

Mother of Red Mountains

A Novel of a Woman's Journey Through Revolutionary China
© 2024

An ambitious civil engineer desperately wants to protect her baby girls in the shadow of China's tumultuous mid-20th century. Despite tragedies in her childhood, Jun crafts a stable life by changing her name twice to fit in a male-dominated and politically charged society. Ambitious and high-achieving in her career, she seeks help from her in-laws to care for the girls. But the in-laws' capitalist class makes them all prime targets for the Red Guards at the onset of the Cultural Revolution in 1966. Jun worries about the well-being of her toddler girls, as they constantly witness their grandparents, and their own safety, being violated. Will Jun triumph over the grave danger she encounters and successfully protect and maintain a stable life for herself and her babies?

"Historical fiction/drama at its finest." - **Pikasho Deka**

"Lucid storytelling." - **Carmen Tenorio**

"I was transferred into this character and went through this journey with her." - **Harley Grace**

"The emotions feel universal and timeless." - **Hopper**

Las Crosses

An Unwavering Journey to a New Life in America © 2023

Fleeing the aftermath of the Tiananmen Square crackdown in 1989 and fueled by a burning desire for a better life, Apple embarks on a daring journey to pursue her doctoral education in America. With no backup plan, Apple must make this journey work. But she has no idea that her starting place, Las Cruces, NM, is a quiet desert town - a far cry from the bustling metropolis she envisioned. Anxious, ignorant, and homesick, Apple faces challenges she never had before. But she is determined to be open-minded. Excited and curious, will she simply survive the fish-out-of-the-water situation many immigrants experience, or will she thrive in this unexpected American adventure?

"A story of opportunity, bravery and self-invention that's as suspenseful and inspiring as it is quintessentially American." **- Jonathan Dee**

"Powerfully depicts scenes, characters, and emotions with bits of comedy." **- Cate McGowen**

"An enjoyable and essential read on cultural contrast from a historical era." **- Ginnah Howard**

"An inspiring story of resilience, hope and joyful curiosity, even in the face of uncertainty and difficulty. Uplifting!" **– Diane Pienta**

28 Voices

Voices Heard Anthology Series, Vol. 1 © 2024

Every life is a story, and every story holds a lesson. Within these 28 intimate essays, a diverse group of authors invites you to witness their most defining moments. They recount the laughter and pain of childhood memories, the forks in the road that marked life-changing events, and the heart's journey through love and relationships. Feel the awe of childbirth and parenthood, the struggle of balancing family and professional ambition, and the courage it takes to adapt to a new culture. With raw honesty, they explore the quiet resilience found in coping with losses and the personal paths to spirituality. These 28 honest reflections on the journey of life is a testament to what we can all learn, and what we have to give.

"Not gonna lie, some of these short stories really got to me. They're worth checking, just prepare yourself." - **Paul Hoon**

"Some of these stories are difficult to get through due to the nature of the stories, but overall the anthology was a good read." - **Jake Jacob**

"Written by ordinary people leading ordinary lives. How very relatable it is. I was enthralled by the talent that was gathered together to contribute to this book. I enjoyed it completely and I strongly recommend it." - **Shannon Brennan**

37 More Voices

Voices Heard Anthology Series, Vol. 2 © 2025

Beyond the everyday, what hidden wisdom awaits in the tapestry of our lives? Picking up where Volume 1, *28 Voices*, left off, this captivating second collection of essays invites you on a profound exploration of discovery and reflection.

Through a diverse array of personal narratives, these pages delve into the myriad ways we learn and grow. From the quiet revelations of self-awareness to the complex dynamics of family and friendship, discover the profound impact of connection. Uncover unexpected insights from the loyalty of pets, the discipline of hobbies, and the expansive perspectives gained from travel and exploration. Ultimately, these essays illuminate how every experience—large or small—contributes to the ever-evolving landscape of our personal philosophies and worldviews.

Join us on a journey of introspection that celebrates the richness of life's lessons, beautifully told.

All-in-One Dotted Journal Notebook

For a Busy, Productive & Mindful Life © 2023

Planners + Organizers + To-dos + Reminders + Trackers + Journals + Random Notes + Doodles + Nuggets of Goodness.

Do you have a busy life? Do you want to be productive? Do you want to have an efficient assistant to provide notes when you need it? Do you want to eliminate loose papers and memos? Do you want to have fewer notebooks or journals to deal with daily? Do you want to spend minimum time preparing your templates and more time to be productive and enjoy life? This All-in-One Dotted Journal Notebook might be just what you need.

Give this a try for one month. There is no need to waste money if it does not work for you. You can find examples to guide you to developing your own habits and uses.

"Takes getting organized to a new level!" - **Joseph Brennan**

"I absolutely love this planner! If you're looking for an efficient planner, this is worth considering." - **Angela Dorris**

"I appreciate most about this notebook is the upfront guidance and examples. It inspired me to use the notebook in ways I never would have thought of." - **Leon Edward**

"I am pleased with the large number of flexible templates for my various needs." - **Kateryna Hlushchenko**

About the Author

Apple An is an award-winning author and professor whose stories explore migration, cultural memory, and the quiet strength of women through times of upheaval. She writes under her pen name to celebrate her Chinese heritage and share universal truths. Apple lives in New York State, where she balances storytelling, scholarship, and a lifelong love of movement and learning. Learn more about Apple An and her creative work at AppleAnBooks.com.